ASK THE DARK

HENRY TURNER

HOUGHTON MIFFLIN HARCOURT

BOSTON   NEW YORK

For information about permission to reproduce selections from this book, write to trade.permissions@hmhco.com or to Permissions, Houghton Mifflin Harcourt Publishing Company, 3 Park Avenue, 19th Floor, New York, New York 10016.

www.hmhco.com

The text was set in Garamond 3 LT Standard.

The Library of Congress has cataloged the hardcover edition as follows:
Turner, Henry, 1962–
Ask the dark / Henry Turner.
p. cm.
Summary: "A thriller about Billy Zeets, a 14-year-old semi-delinquent in a deadly tango with a killer"—Provided by publisher.
[1. Heroes—Fiction. 2. Kidnapping—Fiction. 3. Murder—Fiction. 4. Conduct of life—Fiction. 5. Family problems—Fiction. 6. Mystery and detective stories.] I. Title.
PZ7.1.T877Ask 2015
[Fic]—dc23
2014027737

ISBN: 978-0-544-30827-5 hardcover
ISBN: 978-0-544-81353-3 paperback

Manufactured in the United States of America
DOC 10 9 8 7 6 5 4 3 2 1
4500604850

For my wife, Alma, and our son, Hugo

PART ONE

CHAPTER ONE

I feel better now. I can move my arm some, and walk around a bit. Ache in my belly's still there, but the doctor says it'll go too. Says there's almost nothing that can hurt a fifteen-year-old boy forever, and I'll grow out of that pain like I grow out of a pair of old shoes.

Loads of people have asked me 'bout what happened. Police and doctors and just about everybody in the neighborhood. I never had so many visitors. Tell the truth, I'm tired of getting asked. I feel like just getting on with what's happening now, and not thinking of what's gone by. I want to answer everybody all at once and get it all the hell over with.

But there's one big thing—where to begin.

Because you don't know me.

1

Maybe you seen me on the streets walking around, or riding Old Man Pedersen's bike if you was ever up at night. I mean that girls' bike with the tassels on it. Or maybe you just seen me hanging round Shatze's Pharmacy.

But really knowing me, few people do.

Sam Tate does. He's a boy my age, and he said something true. He come up here to my room the other day and we talked, not just 'bout what happened, but 'bout other things too, things we did together before all this big mess. He was sitting near my bed, right there on the windowsill, looking out the window at the trees. Then he looked at me and said, *The real thing is, you'd never have done it, never even found out about it, if you hadn't done all the things people hated you for. It turns out those were the right things to do, Billy. Isn't that funny? All that stealing and never going to school. It's what made it so you were outside a lot, seeing things nobody else saw. Hidden and secret things.*

He was dead-on right with what he said. I laughed. I saved three boys, so they tell me. Got beat and shot doin' it. And Sam says I'd never of done it, 'cept I was always stealing and busting things, and creeping around people's yards at night. That is funny.

But I s'pose it's true.

I don't ride that girls' bike no more. Got a new one. There it is, leaning against the wall over there, bright and shiny. Got twenty-one gears, so I'm told. I'll have to figure that out. How to use'm. Man that brought it was Jimmy Brest's father, the Colonel, USMC. He wheeled it in, laughing and smiling. My daddy was with him a minute, then left and it was just the Colonel and me. And you know what he did? He come over to the bed and took my hand, and he called me the bravest boy he'd ever known, for what I done to save his son. He said I was a hero, and he was quiet a minute, and was almost gonna cry.

But that's like everybody. It seems no matter who gets wind of what I done, from my sister or Sam Tate or one of them news shows on TV, they all start bawling their heads off. So I figure I best tell it myself and get things straight.

'Cause I don't want to make nobody cry. 'Specially colonels, USMC.

The fact is, I ain't no hero, and I aim to prove it. What I done, if I done anything, was get my daddy a fruit stand. See, my daddy was feeling bad and needed money and couldn't do for hisself, so I done it. And to tell this right you gotta know about that, and other things too, like about us losing the house and what my sister done to get herself to be having a baby. You gotta know all that, 'cause if you do, everything else I say will make sense. Sort'f add up, know what I mean?

I ain't hardly left my bed in four weeks, just hanging

around my room. I couldn't stand lookin' out the window no more and seeing the days and nights come and go, I was goin' crazy. So I got one of them video games. Hand-held. Sam Tate brought it. What you do with it is move this little monkey through a maze and traps. Monkey's gotta jump and roll and bounce, and if he don't make it he falls through a gap and you gotta start over. You use these little buttons to make him jump. Thing makes beeping noises. Plays a little tune if you do it right.

Can you imagine being that little monkey? Jumping and rolling all day? I kept thinking I was him, and I got so bothered by it, what with whipping my fingers all over it and my eyes jiggling, that I threw the damn thing out the window and heard it bust on the ground.

So now I'm in trouble again 'cause I got no idea what I'm gonna tell Sam Tate.

Since I busted that monkey game I got me a little TV, my daddy brung it up here to me. I started watching that all the time, and just this morning I saw something that explains pretty good why I decided to go 'head and tell all this. There was this talk show on, one with the big fat lady who always got guests on with problems like Welfare and drinking and drugs and whatnot, usually yelling and screaming and hitting each other right there on the show till cops come out and arrest'm, which I can't say is real or not, or if they just getting paid money to say all them things. But this morning she had on a lady who went through cancer and divorce and all sorts of troubles, only to get rich decoratin' folks' houses, famous folks, after she was on her feet again. Anyway, this lady said that even on her darkest day, she always had her dream that kept her going when nothing else did.

Now that's just like me. Just like me'n the fruit stand. 'Cause when all this was going on and I was trying to make all that money to save the house, I don't think a day went by that I didn't say to myself, *I gotta get that fruit stand! Gotta get my daddy that damn fruit stand.*

Scuze my language.

After the lady told 'bout her dream, she said one more thing. I liked it.

She said, *If I did it, you can too!*

That's just how I feel. And that's why I ain't no hero. If I did it, you can too. 'Cause I ain't better'n nobody.

So here goes.

CHAPTER TWO

The first boy got took last September, just a week after school began. I knew him, boy named Tommy Evans, he was fourteen then, same as me. We didn't get along too good. I 'member once he caught up with me in an alley over behind them shops on Fister Street and he started whaling away on me, mostly chest and back, yelling some shit 'bout how I stole his bookbag and threw it in a dumpster and someone saw me do it. But that someone was lying his ass off, 'cause I never stole it. Stole Evans's jacket one day, off a bench at a park over near Dayton Avenue. That I done 'cause I heard he was sayin' nasty things 'bout me, but he never knew 'cause I tossed it down and he found it, so he was hitting me for nothing.

Anyway, after I run I went by his house, running kind of weak 'cause my chest and back was full of bruises, and I hove a brick at his house. Not just brick, cinder block. Damned thing weighed so much it fell out my hands and hit my foot. Didn't break nothing, 'cept the pain made me so mad I got it up and hove it again. But that didn't mean much, 'cause that cinder block was heavier than a motherfucker and I only threw it 'bout three/four foot.

Scuze my language.

'Cept for stuff like that I never knew him much. Ain't like we went to the same school'r nothing, or hung round any the same places. I mean, a couple boys round my way really can't stand me and spend a lot of time just thinking up fresh ways to kick my ass. But this Tommy Evans, he weren't that sort, and prob'ly didn't like me 'cause'f how I'm in trouble all the time, and his parents prob'ly told'm I ain't the right sort of boy for him to know.

Anyway, he got took they say when he was walking home from school. Different people say they seen him last. There was Mrs. Steinwitz, who runs the grocery. Said she seen him, sold him a candy bar or something. Then a lady named Jenkins, whose son he knew, was out scrubbing her porch rail spars and she said she seen him too, and also seen the car that picked him up. But on her life she couldn't remember that car, or truck, or van, 'cause each time the cops asked her she seemed to think it was something different.

Anyway, that's how it began. At the time I was in seventh grade the second time, like I still gonna be, and I spent most of my time downtown at school and didn't get much news 'bout what happens up our way, 'cause my teachers down there're just a bunch'f nuns and they ain't never had much to tell me, 'cept to say I got stains on my soul.

But Evans getting snatched made news all over. So on weekends I was going out with Marvin and hanging posters now instead of the sales flyers from Shatze's, Shatze's Pharmacy, where I go sometimes for work. Usually with Marvin I just drive beside him in the delivery van 'cause his leg is bad, I mean his foot with the big shoe on it, and he don't like getting out of the van. So I do it. When we make deliveries he gives me half the tip and when we dump flyers he pays me a buck'n hour, which ain't good but I like talking with'm, so it's fair. He an old black man, Marvin is, and got his bad foot in a war somewhere, and when the time's right I'll let you know more 'bout him.

Them weekends, first ones after Tommy Evans got took, we hung posters. I mean posters of Tommy Evans, and I know you seen'm. They the ones with MISSING printed under that school picture of Tommy's face and the date and some details. Just like on milk cartons and them flyers you get in the mail and throw away. But they never found him. Posters didn't help, and when the snows come with winter they got all mulched and soaked away to bits with just the tape left on phone poles and walls where I used to hang'm.

Next boy got took was Tuckie Brenner, twelve years old. Him I didn't know. First thing I thought driving around with Marvin was how funny his name was on the posters. I mean, who the hell names their boy Tuckie Brenner? Course, that ain't the worst I ever heard. Worst was this boy Billy Hill, he was in school with me. When the nun called out his name she done it last name first, so it come out *Hill, Billy*. Can you imagine that? Hillbilly. Shit. We all laughed, it was morning and we was at assembly in the gym, whole school was there, and even though on the next mornings every day the nun said different and called his name *Hill, William,* it didn't matter and the boys called out, *Hillbilly!* 'cause who could ever forget that? So old Billy Hill, he didn't last long in that school of mine.

Anyhow, this Tuckie Brenner, he got took four/five months after Tommy Evans. They say he was playing in a field round the time of sundown when it happened, wintertime. Other boys he was with left him to go home and so he was alone, and that's the last anybody seen him, 'cept they found a scarf he was wearing lying on the ground later. Marvin and me, we hung posters again but 'cause nobody ever found Tommy Evans it felt like a waste of time.

After Tuckie got took the whole neighborhood went a little crazy. Everybody was scared and putting up fences and new locks on their doors and some boys said their daddies bought guns and such. And no boy my age or older, up to eighteen, was allowed out after dark. Curfew, they called it. And even though there weren't no curfew in the daytime there was a lot more police cars in the neighborhood, and we was s'posed to walk round only in groups of three or more if we could manage it.

Round the time all that started I was still staying up nights. Couldn't sleep since my mother'd died, about two years back. Most nights I'd be up till morning, 'cause my thoughts bothered me, and I couldn't make'm stop.

But just lying in bed made me antsy. So I started going out. I'd see them little branch shadows waving on the sheet hung over my window, sort of calling me away. Then I'd get up. Floors might creak, so I can't walk the halls—I climb out the window. I hold tight to the shutters and crawl around. I pass my daddy's window and there he is under the covers, a lump in the dark.

House used to be apartments, so there's a fire escape out back, made'f wood. Wouldn't do any good in a fire, burn right up, but it's great for climbing. Down at bottom I'd run crost the yard to the alley and in a minute I'm free.

I'd keep real quiet and hear the wind whistle through the trees, and cars swish by out front, and sometimes even the ring of a train far away. I never had to worry 'bout getting seen, 'cause at three or four in the morning ain't nobody out but me.

Most nights I just stayed in the neighborhood. Nothing was going on. Just houses dark and yards empty. Course it was scary at first. I even creeped around the woods in places so dark I felt maybe I should run on home. But it weren't too long afore I was used to it, and would go anywhere no matter how scared I got.

Like I said, I started doing this after my mother died, two years back in springtime, and at first I stayed close to home. But when summer came I got all bold and sometimes snagged my neighbor's bike to ride downtown, going through side streets and alleys so cops won't see me and ask me why I'm out so late. I loved it down there, with the buildings quiet and hardly a car going by anywhere, but all the streetlights still on and me riding through the cool wind. City was all my own. And thinking didn't hurt so much like when I was lying in bed.

You can imagine how it got in my way when the curfew come a couple years later. But I still snuck out some nights. And it was funner than ever before. Because now the curfew was up it felt different at night, more dangerous for sure, but real wild too, know what I mean? 'Cause since them boys got took I knew something bad was out there in the dark. And that gave me a feeling. Sort'f like a tingly feeling I get when I know something's up for sure.

A few months after Tuckie got took I went out early while it was still dark and ran down to the woods. I was headed to this man's house I know, man who leaves his lawn mower out in his yard all night. He don't never use it, so I figured I'd take it away, maybe make a go-kart out of't, real electric go-kart like some boys have, with a wood frame and metal sidings.

Coming 'long the trail, branches batted my face, and soon my feet was sloshin' in my shoes all wet from the grass. I went down crost the stream and then uphill to where the houses was, huge houses all lost in the trees, behind a big stone wall higher'n my head. Moss on them stones was slippery from dew, and I smacked myself good on the elbow climbing over, and then tossed down to the other side where I crouched low lookin' round the dark.

I didn't see the mower. So I went over to the toolshed and looked in the window that had glass with chicken wire in it that don't break, reinforced glass. There it was, right inside. Mower, I mean. I could just barely see it in the little red light glowing off some tool chargers.

I tried the door but the old man had locked it good, and that made the whole walk through them woods worth nothing at all, 'cept for scaring the shit outta me. I was wet, besides, 'cause the dew had soaked my pants and shoes, and my face was all scratched up and bleeding from cutting through brambles in the dark.

So I went back. It was getting light, and I was coming through the woods toward the stream. I was right below where the wood-chip trail cuts over the field up from where the stream gully is, and there're some big houses farther up, behind big trees.

Then I stopped.

A boy lay on the bank of the stream. He was naked, that boy, 'cept one shoe, with his body on the sand and rocks but his head partways in the water, the hair waving like weeds in the stream. He lay on his chest but his head was turned to the side and I saw his face good, all covered in cuts and blood.

I looked a long while, but I didn't say a word, or yell out.

It was Tommy Evans.

I seen a piece of paper sticking all red and bright to his dead, naked ass. I walked over real lightly, stone to stone

13

and not leaving no marks in the sand. I figured if it was me lying there I wouldn't want no trash sticking to my ass for any and all to see. So I bent over and snatched it up. I knew I couldn't just throw it over once I touched it, so I put it in my pocket. Paper stuck to my fingers a second when I did that, 'cause glue was on it. Then I crost the stream and climbed a tree real high, till nobody could see me, but I could see everything, peeking down through the leaves and branches.

I figure it was 'bout six when a jogger ran by huffin' and puffin', steam comin' out his mouth. But he didn't see nothing. A little after that came one of them goody-two-shoes families, out to pick up litter so's to keep the woods neat. They dawdled on the wood-chip trail, picking here and picking there, stuffin' what they got in trash bags. The kids was dressed for camp in little uniforms, and their daddy wore a gray suit and everything else for work, 'cept his feet and pants legs was stuffed in galoshes. They didn't come near the stream, though. When they was gone I had to take a leak and did it down through the branches, making no noise at all.

Then a lady came out from a house I could just see through the trees, and she came down to the water. When she saw, she screamed her head off, running back up to her house.

I climbed down and ran. No one saw me. I knew it wouldn't be five minutes 'fore the police was there, swarmin' all round, and damned if I'll be stuck up in a tree all day.

I took a trail that headed for a street. Walking along I swat branches, and let'm swat back at my face just for fun, and it hurt a little. I stuffed my hand in my pocket and felt that piece of paper. *Well, at least I got the trash off'm,* I thought, and I made to toss it away, but that didn't seem right. So I hung on to it, squeezing it twixt my fingers.

I was thinking back on how Tommy Evans used to call me nasty names, bad ones. Shit. I wouldn't care now what all names he'd call me, if he could get up and walk around again. But cut up like he was, I knew that couldn't happen.

I come out the woods at them two towers where the college students live behind their school, dormitories. I had to ford the stream, climb a hill, and climb a wire fence, right up over the barbed wire. Then I let down and crost the parking lots, slinking 'tween the cars and looking inside. But I didn't see nothing I wanted and didn't even try the doors, which all was locked anyways, prob'ly. So I went crost the lots and up the street, into where's all the houses is in the neighborhood all lost in trees.

CHAPTER THREE

This the same day the letter came, but I weren't home then. I was feeling too riled to go home 'cause I seen Tommy Evans, found him, I mean, though I never told it till now, 'cause wouldn't you'f wondered why I was in them woods so early in the first place? That's why I never told it.

I wanted to see what I might hear 'bout it before going home, who they think might'f done it and so on. One place to do that was Shatze's, so I figured I'd head up'ere, running through backyards and alleys. But afore I got there I seen Richie Harrigan goin' by in that old pickup he drives. He yells, Hey, Monkey Boy, come ride with me! And I figure I might learn more drivin' round with him than hanging round Shatze's with Marvin, so's I went over and got on in.

We drove around back alleys looking for what we

could salvage in yards, and asking neighbors what they had in their garages we could maybe take away. Some of them alleys are real narrow, and driving through'm in Richie's pickup the branches was smacking on the windshield like to break it, and the tires was bumpin' over the broken ground, so we inside was bouncin' crazy on our asses, damn near smacking our heads on the window frames.

But we didn't find nothing.

Finally Richie had this idea to go check out the big fields behind his old high school 'cause there'd be cans there to bag up and recycle, maybe make a buck off that. I knew that was time to quit. I knew 'cause I'd done it before with'm, and once he started picking up cans and bottles he'd go on to other junk like old tires and empty boxes and anything he could get his hands on, thinking maybe he could sell it for scrap, but really thinking it was his turn to go pickin' up the whole damn neighborhood, like it's some sacred duty he got to get it all clean.

So I went home.

First he drove me not too far from his house, which ain't nowhere near my house, me in the truck bed now 'cause he wants me to hold down this mess of loose posters he found on the street. We did hear about Tommy from some people we saw, parents on lawns, mainly, who we was asking for junk. They said he was found and he was dead, and it was sad to hear it. More'n sad, really. Horrible. But there weren't no word on who done it.

So there I was up Richie's way and I gotta walk home. That Richie, he got money—I mean his daddy has it—but me, I live on this one skinny little street about a mile from him, where people who ain't got so much live. I was walking feeling that piece of paper in my pocket, same one I got off Tommy Evans, because I tell you my mind was sort of stuck on him, and wondering who the hell might'f killed him. Because I didn't really tell you how he looked. His face, I mean. And I ain't gonna tell you. But it weren't something a person does, I mean no regular sane person.

Second day of summer vacation. Hot. Bright. Me, I'm walking through the neighborhood with a nice breeze blowin' in the trees, and sunlight shining off the house fronts as I go passin' by. Tell the truth, when my mind got off Tommy, I was feeling pretty good, especially since I'd dodged Richie, who by now was prob'ly up to his waist in weeds digging up trash like a crazy man, for no special reason at all.

Then I passed the house, and that should'f clued me. Should'f let me know what might be up at home.

See, about a year ago—no, more'n that, two years ago, now that fall's come round again—was just when my daddy was painting that house.

I stopped and come up to it, it all quiet and neat and now painted perfect, where before it had looked haunted with rusty window screens and tarpaper peeling off the roof and dead leaves everywhere. Perfect it was, and I looked at it, the sun shining down and the cool breeze on me. I looked at the eave, the top one there, up by them box-windows three in a row.

I'm talking now about the time just after my mother died, when all them bills was coming. Doctor bills. First there was just what they call "deductible," then the whole thing went crazy because the insurance company stopped paying at all. Make ends meet my daddy took on more work. He was working too much, sometimes going at two jobs a day, say eight hours on a house job, then maybe four after dark and by lamplight, going over a fence or shoring up a pipe or you name it.

That eave up there, that's where it happened. My daddy was out painting one night, there where that little piece of roof give just enough inches for a foothold. He took a step back, and *pow!* Tripped on a power cord, all snagged up. Fell off that roof. Hit bushes down at bottom. Messed up his back good—fractured the spine.

After that he's in the hospital. Can't pay. So next up came the mortgage. Second mortgage. My daddy owned the house. Paid for it by workin' all his life. But a man came

19

to him and told'm it's worth a damn sight more'n what he paid, and with a second mortgage he could make hospital payments.

I'd like to shoot that man.

Anyway, he did that, my daddy, to pay up best he could. But it weren't enough. And while all this was happening and my mother's funeral expenses come and Daddy can't work at all no more, we start going out to Social Services.

Welfare. Medical. You name it. Little offices where all you do is wait forever and when somebody do come out to see you, they never give you what you want and look at you like you ain't washed your clothes.

So I just stood there. Lookin' at that house. I thought maybe there was some kind of secret there. Some kind of answer. The eaves and the drainpipes and the gutters looked all complicated like a riddle.

But there weren't no answer. Just wood and tarpaper.

I walked on. Didn't think about it. Just kept going. Walked along the sidewalks and half hour later I come up the stairs to our place and went inside.

Straight back's the kitchen, that's where Daddy was sitting. Sittin' still, squat, and gray, not moving, letter on the table. I come in, amble past, and get a drink of water at the sink. He don't move at all. It's dark in there 'cause the window curtains is drawn, but he don't open'm, I do.

I say, How're you, Daddy?

He don't answer for a while. I'm leaning on the sink, drinking my water, and he says, They're taking the house.

How so?

He ain't looking at me, just staring down at the letter. He got his glasses on, ones that bug his eyes. I can't pay, he says. Missed too many payments. Now they want it all. Foreclosure. We have three months. Pay or quit.

Uh-huh, I say.

I stare at him a minute. Then I go upstairs and lie on my bed.

Ten minutes later my sister, Leezie, come in. I didn't look up. I was staring at a little patch of wall, just staring at it, place where the plaster's all flaky.

She says, Billy, we gotta help Daddy.

I know, I said.

We can't lose the house, Billy.

Um-hmm.

I felt her come closer, lean over me. Though I didn't look up and she didn't make no noise.

Can you do it, Billy?

I gave a little laugh. I said, Leezie, you sixteen and can get a job. Why put it all on me?

I couldn't never make so much alone, she said. Anyhow, Billy, you got ways. She talked real quiet.

21

I stared at that flaky place. Didn't want to answer. *I got ways?* I wondered if she knew what she was askin' me.

Then I said, I'll try.

You promise?

I felt her standing there, waiting.

It took me a minute, but I said yeah. Then I looked up at her.

Will you do something for me? I said. Go down ask'm what he owes?

She murmured yes and walked away. I could barely hear her. Footsteps soft as breath.

Room was empty now. Everything felt still.

Minute later she came back.

Forty-eight, she said.

I rolled over on my back.

Thousand?

Yes, Leezie said, swallowing a catch in her voice.

Don't cry, I said.

I won't, she said.

She bent down and kissed me. Then I heard the door close.

I lay there. Looking at the ceiling.

Forty-eight thousand.

God fuckin' damn.

Scuze my language.

CHAPTER FOUR

Next day I got up early. Was thinking. I been saddled with a lot in my time. Seen crazy shit, ain't lyin'.

But forty-eight thousand was something new.

I got up thinking about it, put my clothes on thinking about it, and ate my breakfast without it never leaving my mind.

How the hell I gonna do it? I had no goddamn idea.

I went out. Wandered. Went through alleys and streets looking around. But there was nothing. Just lawn furniture and junk on porches. Nothing worth forty-eight thousand.

Saw Richie Harrigan in his pickup, drivin' slow down the street under the trees, and he waved at me. Hey, Monkey Boy, climb in, he said.

Monkey Boy, yeah, that's what he calls me. You'll see why.

I did. I sat and he said he got a job for a man on Frederick Street, man in a big house. Says he's going to the HomeWorld Lumber, gotta buy supplies, will I come with'm?

Shit yeah, I say. Sure ain't got nothing better to do.

We drove. Went through the neighborhood and then out on some route, I don't know the number. Summer was going good now and all the woods 'longside the route had that foamy sort of lime-green color, you know it? Outside, cars was whizzing by.

Richie, he's smoking a cigarette, window open, listening to the radio, some country singer. He's big, Richie. Not tall, but big arms, big chest. Burly, I mean. Short hair and looks neat, 'cept all his teeth are brown'n busted. From when he was drinking, I s'pose.

Titans gonna win the pennant this year I bet, you know that? he says, looking forward.

That's a year off, I said.

Bet they do, he said. They got some good players coming up. He nods his head and grins, thinking 'bout it.

He'd know. Used to be captain of the Titans, his old football team—quarterback, he was, and got a scholarship to boot. Ten years back. Folks say he used to look good, drivin' in a convertible, girls just stuffed in it, all fawnin' on him. Say he used to be rich. Wouldn't know it now. He told me what happened to'm. I'll tell you too, but not just now.

When we got to the store I took a cart from outside and went in. Richie walked beside me in the aisles, holding a list in his hand with what he needs scribbled on it.

So I say, Richie, I need forty-eight thousand dollars.

He sort'f just stops right there and looks at me.

What the hell for? he says.

My daddy's gonna lose the house, I say.

Hold up a minute, he says, and moving aside he gets one of them ladders with wheels on it and brings it over. Okay, Monkey Boy, climb up there, he says.

Now you know why he calls me Monkey Boy. He don't never climb no ladder, has me do it. Makes him dizzy, so he says, something left over from back when he was drinkin'.

I climb and he watches, and when I'm up top I look down and ask what he wants.

You gotta see my daddy, Richie says. Gimme those nails, flatheads, the two-and-a-halfs.

I read the numbers and grab a bag.

Here goes—flatheads, I say. Why's that?

He runs banks, Richie says.

I hand him down the nails.

Makes a lot of money, he says. Hell of a lot more than what you're after.

He ain't gonna see me, I said.

Why not?

'Cause what I done to his car. What you need now?

Them eyebolts. Thought you paid for that?

Nope. Never did, I said.

I climb down and wheel the cart over to the aisle where they got concrete and plaster. Richie, he brings the ladder.

Gimme that bag of plaster, too, will ya, Monkey Boy? Big one.

Got it, I said.

Damn thing's heavy. But I lug it.

Come see him, Richie says. See him at the bank. He's there all day.

You mean a loan? I climb down beside him.

Yeah, that's one way, he says. You just gotta have collateral. Push the cart, will ya?

I start pushing the cart. I push fast and make motor noises and yell, *Beep beep!* like I'm a truck and if I gotta back up I make the other beeping sound and say, Hold up, hold up, and Richie's there right beside me, laughing. What's collateral? I ask.

Something you put up against the money you get, he says.

That's what my daddy already done, I say. I ain't doing that mess come nothing.

Well, then there's credit, Richie says. That they just give ya. But you gotta be eighteen.

Eighteen? That's too far off for me, I say. I need the money *now*.

Richie laughs. Then you best get a job, he says. *Good* one.

I'm trying, I say. And I push the cart to check out.

CHAPTER FIVE

So that's what I done.

Tried to find a job.

It was still early after I left Richie, just 'bout eleven. So I went around. I tried the grocery store up on the avenue, Lowry's, I tried the cleaners on Burton Way. I went to the gas station there on Bellsprint, and crost over the street where they got that little market run by the Chinese lady. They all said no. Mr. Potecki, who cuts meat up the grocery, he told me to get out. Knows me 'cause I go to school with 'is daughter and I got her once to hook school with me, and she got caught.

By the time I was done I felt real beat, so I took a drink of water from a yard hose and lay down on the grass.

Grass got me thinking, so I got up. Went and rung

the doorbell. *Hey, Mr. So-and-So, you need your lawn mowed?* Shakes head, says no. I try twenty other places. Finally get one. It's a lady in her apron cleaning house, and she sort'f thinks about it a minute with her eyes rolling around, then smiles and takes me on.

She got this power mower, and the wheels are s'posed to turn by themselves, but something was busted or going the wrong way, 'cause I had to push hard as I could to keep that thing moving.

I go extra careful, 'specially out back round this big wood kiddie house she built, or her husband built, for their kid, boy I know named Joey, 'cause it got nice paint and she don't want no scratches.

Sun was hot, and pretty soon I'm wet head to foot with sweat, both shirt and pants, and when it's all done I still got to go around with snips, 'cause the truth is what with having to push the mower, the path I went was scraggly with plenty of high grass in the gaps between.

When I get finished, the lady she comes back out and checks what I done, then gives me the twelve bucks I'd asked her for.

I think about that for a minute. Twelve bucks down makes it forty-seven thousand nine hundred eighty-eight.

To go.

I don't know how many little yards it would take, so I

start thinking 'bout how big the yard would have to be for me to make it all in one go, and I figure 'bout the size of Delaware.

I got done there at around three thirty and still had a few hours left before curfew. I'm thinking I need more money, twelve bucks ain't gonna cut it. So I figure I best go down Shatze's and see'f Marvin's around.

Now, I gotta stop right here and say something. 'Cause comin' up I'm gonna tell you the first thing I saw that helped me find those boys and the man who took'm.

But you gotta understand one thing.

I didn't know what I was seeing.

Least not right then, when I first seen it.

Now some people say that makes me pretty dumb, because what with all I *did* see, then and a couple weeks later, they say it wouldn't be hard to know just what it all was and put it all together.

Well that might be true. But looking back now at what horrors I seen that still wakes me up some nights in cold sweats, I figure maybe I wish I was even dumber than I was, and never noticed nothing in the first place.

And let me tell you something else, too. You know what was going on at home for me and what I needed to do, I mean make all that money and with only ninety days to do it.

So that's what I was thinking about, the house and the money, because no way I tried could I forget it. It was always pushing me on. And maybe if something like that was pushing you, you wouldn't be so smart yourself, and miss a few things when you seen'm, till you got a chance to add'm all up later on.

I got to Shatze's round four o'clock and I seen Marvin all ready with a heap of white bags on the counter. I asked'm'f I could tag along and he said sure so I grabbed the bags. Big armload they was, and with Marvin holding the door for me I went out, past that old fat counter lady, Miss Norris, looking nasty at me over the counter, 'cause she caught me taking candy once. I go round back, and there's the van. Marvin follows, limping on that busted foot he got, and I dump the bags in the bin between the seats and sit. Marvin, he gets in beside me and starts up the motor.

We drive a bit, wind blowing over us 'cause that van's the sort that ain't got no doors and you gotta watch your ass not to fall out. Marvin's got the list of addresses he wrote in his hand on the steering wheel, and I watch the houses and yards and the sun bright over everything, people walking their dogs or just standing in their gardens and the birds singing everywhere.

Then I turn to Marvin.

Shit's going on, ain't it? I say.

He nods.

Yup, he says. Sure is. *Lots* of shit. *Nothing* but shit. *Same* old shit.

He says that all the time. Same old shit, I mean. S'where he's coming from.

They found Tommy Evans, I say. He was beat up bad, I hear. Ain't a good way to go.

No way's a good way, Marvin says. You just make sure *you* don't go getting in no strange man's car, you hear me?

I hear you, I said.

I was looking up the street at how the sunshine came down through the trees and leaves and still looked green on the black of the street, same color like the leaves.

Then I say, Marvin, I need forty-eight thousand dollars.

He looks at me, eyes buggin'. What the hell for?!

Bank's taking my daddy's house, I said.

For a second he don't say nothing. Then he looks at me. *Shit,* he says. You mean *your* house.

Same one, I said.

God'amn, Marvin says, sort'f breathes. Looks at me. Why can't your daddy make it?

He's too bad hurt, I said. Fell off that roof, remember?

God'amn, he says again. That's some mean nasty shit you got coming down on you. Some *mean* nasty shit.

Uh-huh, I said. But I gotta make it. Th'money, I mean. Promised Leezie. Ain't got no ideas, though. Least no good ones.

Now Marvin, he looks at me, and I know what he's thinkin', can just tell from the squint of his eyes.

And he says, You ain't gonna start slippin', is you?

Slippin' where? I say, but I know what he's talking about.

Back to where you was a couple years ago, he says. You was a *crazy* kid, Billy. Actin' out every way, saying you was here when you was really there and stealing everything that ain't nailed down! Used to scare even me, and I'm a man who *done* some crazy shit in his day. Boy, back then I wouldn't've even let you in the van with me, you was so damn wild. So don't you slip. I don't want to see you in jail or no boys' home, you understand?

I was smiling now, looking at'm. I said, Naw. Ain't slippin'. I swore.

How swore?

To my mother, afore she died, I said. On her grave, too.

He looked at me a minute, eyes right on me, his face

all empty now 'cause the feeling run out of it. I weren't smiling no more, neither.

Well that's good, Billy, Marvin says. I know what all that meant to you, seeing her pass. Seen the change in you myself, if nobody else round here did. So don't go slippin' now that trouble's come. Listen. I been in shit myself years back, *deep* shit. No money, no job, and children, too. But it all comes right in the end. You gotta believe that, and hold yourself together.

It felt good hearing him say all that, so I promised I would. Of course, me I'm thinking, I went after that mower—was that slippin'? Didn't tell about finding Tommy, what about that? Hell, worst of all is I go and promise Leezie I gonna get forty-eight thousand—and to get that done right is like askin' for a *world* of slippin'.

I guess hearing 'bout the house riled'm—Marvin, I mean—'cause after a minute he pounds the steering wheel and says, *Shit!* And I *mean* shit. See, that's the thing. Boy like you ain't got money. And your daddy ain't got money, 'specially now that he got hurt and can't go to work and your poor mother died, bless her soul. And if there's one thing I know, nobody gonna dig you out.

That's the truth, I said.

Damn right, Marvin says. Fact is, less you got, the less

you get. And that's true for both black and white. Rich man ain't ever gonna give you nothing, even if you and yours is right outside his doorway starving yourselves to death. 'Specially in this damn neighborhood. Rich folks, they all plain crazy, and that's the god'amn truth.

I hear you, I says.

All this time we talked we was making deliveries, him stopping and me running up, and now we gone to a couple more houses. One of'm I got to tell you about. I mean Simon Hooper's house. You prob'ly seen him around, though he don't get out much, 'cept to walk his dog. I had a whole mess of drugs for 'is mother, who they say lives in the back room and ain't come out her bed in six years, though I never seen her. Say she's big and fat and don't never take a bath, and if she do, it's Simon who helps'r. We all used to make fun of'm for that.

I got outta the van and went up. House is narrow and brown and dirty and covered over with bushes and trees that ain't ever been cut for years, and lots of old dirty junk mud-specked in the yard and ten/twenty old newspapers on the porch, still rubber-banded but the paper looking all mushed and spackered from rain. Big board fence all round the place, higher'n my head, and the house next door, too, this old empty house that I can just see through the trees.

I knock and course the first thing I hear's the dog barking, big huge nasty barks that raise the hair on my arms.

Door opens. There's Simon. Holds the screen door tight. I can see his face just barely through the dirty screen. He about my age. Long face and droopy nose and long hair, real greasy.

Shit. Now I'm thinking 'bout all the times me'n lots of other boys called him names and threw things at him and chased him home, and I'm wishing I could take those times back, 'cause there right with him he got his dog, Bear, he calls'm, holding'm by the scruff of the neck. Damn dog's jaws'r all growly with the skin pulled back and spit going everywhere, and he's the biggest dog I ever saw, head right up to my chest, four foot. Simon, I seen him training Bear in his yard, behind the board fence, and that dog'll do anything he says. Got'm three years ago at a police dog show, and ain't nobody teased him since then, believe me, 'bout giving 'is mother baths'r nothing.

What do you want? Simon asks.

I come from Shatze's, I say, acting like I don't know him even though I know him good. He looks at what I got in my hands, the white bags, then looks at me again with nothing in his eyes and says, Stay there a minute, and closes the door.

I hear him dragging Bear back and the dog's big feet and claws scratching the floor. Then it's all quiet and I stand there all alone, waiting and looking down into Hooper's yard, smelling busted-up acorns and brown leaves, a sort of dead, dirt smell, all mulched'n soggy, 'cause he prob'ly ain't raked'm up in five/six years.

I back up'n look around. Ain't nobody can see me, 'cause his yard's all full of trees and bushes. I listen for Simon inside but I can't hear nothing. I brung him stuff before, and I know I got plenty of time to wait, 'cause what he gonna do now is go back and get his mother to write a check, and then hunt around for whatever cash they got on hand to tip me. And all that takes forever, 'cause anybody can see by the way they keep house, nothing ever stays in the same place for them to find without going searching for it, fishing under the bed or under stacks of magazines for cash and checkbook both. So real fast I get up on the railing and jump to the board fence. Second later I'm down in the yard, next-door house. I'm thinking about the forty-eight thousand, sure, and wondering if there's anything in there worth taking.

House is empty, like I said. Nobody lives there. I knew that 'cause I went in about a year back and seen nothing but empty rooms. But I couldn't say what might'f happened since. Sometimes these old houses is used for storage by the folks who owns'm, and you never know what you might find. 'Cause you hear stories. Stories about crazy rich people with bed bags full of money, or hunks of gold in old cold furnaces, or certificates and deeds all forgotten about stuffed in drawers not opened for twenty years. And while most of that's plain hooey, sometimes it's for real, too.

I chin up to a window and look in, but I can't see much. Window's covered on the inside with black plastic, prob'ly a trash bag, but one side's loose and I can see just past. Some people been by, yeah, maybe using the house for storage, 'cause there's a pile of old clothes on the floor. Some cardboard boxes, too, pretty big ones, with pictures of tomatoes printed on the sides. But the lids's all closed up so I can't see inside'm. And me, I'm thinkin', *Bingo.* 'Cause while it might not be worth no forty-eight thousand, you ain't never gonna know for sure till you look.

I hear a noise and think maybe Simon's coming back, so fast as I come I'm over that fence again and standing at his door.

Door opens and he's there. Ain't got Bear this time. He unhooks the screen and puts his hands out. Gives me a check and takes the bags. While he does I get a lil' nosy looking past him to see whether what they say about his mother is true. But the house is gloomy and the doors and windows is all shuttered so I can't see nothing 'cept shadows over piles of cluttery junk.

Here, he says, and his hand comes out past the screen door, with a buck in it. I take it and turn and the last I hear he's shut the door and Bear's in there scratching and barking.

CHAPTER SIX

So that's the first time I seen it. The house, I mean, the house I come to call the dark house, 'cause there never was a light on inside. And all I seen in it was just coats and boxes. So I don't care how smart you are, there weren't nothing mysterious, and there sure weren't no way right then for me to know what was *really* inside, hid in the attic and cellar. All's that interested me was them boxes and what might be in'm. I was feelin' real excited, thinkin' there was prob'ly lots more stuff too, upstairs and in other rooms. And even though I'd just had that talk with Marvin, I gotta say, my mind was already workin' on findin' a good time to sneak back in.

Last place we went I saw Richie Harrigan was out front workin' in the next yard, carrying some boxes up on the porch. He waved but couldn't stop and talk 'cause the man he was working for was standing there watching him, bent-looking old man who didn't look too friendly, so I just waved back, and didn't say nothing.

House I'm going to is next door, so I go up. Lady comes to the door and for some reason she wants me to come round back, so I jump down off the porch and slip through the side yard. I get to the back and there she is, old lady 'bout Marvin's age but white, and she takes what I give'r and I get a buck in return.

I'd told Marvin to drive on without me. That was our last delivery, and he said for me to keep whatever tip I got all for myself.

So I go through the backyard gate and out into the alley.

Now, usually, afore just walking out like that, I'd'f checked the way. And I'd'f listened. But I s'pose I didn't care that day or my mind was all cluttered up thinking about that house next door to Hooper's, 'cause by now I was pretty hard-stuck on seein' what was in them boxes.

But I wish I had looked, 'cause right then I heard a boy call out to me, and not too friendly, neither.

Zeets! What the hell are you doing around here? he says.

I look over. I know the boy. It's Jimmy Brest.

For a second I stand there and think maybe I'll run, just dart back through the yard and see'f I can make it out. But he's bigger, and runs faster, so I stay where I am.

Making deliveries, I say. Just done with it.

Haven't you come to *rob* me again? he says, and he grins a little, like that's funny.

I never robbed you, I say.

Bullshit! he says.

He's got in his hands a basketball, been throwing it up to the hoop over the garage door he's standing at, and now he hits that basketball one hard dribble on the ground. It says, *Bap!*

I *know* you did, he says. You stole my bike, you little piece of shit.

Now he stares hard right at me.

I don't say nothing.

Of course, that's just natural, he says, grinning again. It's like your whole family.

Nothing wrong with my family, I say.

Nothing? he says. You're a *redneck.* A *grit.* You, and your father and your sister. Everyone in this neighborhood thinks you're just *trash.* They want you to leave. Why *don't* you leave? You don't have any right to live here. Everyone *hates* you.

Ain't true, I say.

Now, you all know there a lot of people down my way who don't like me. I stole too much and busted up too much to be anything like popular. But if I had one worst enemy in the whole world it was this boy, Jimmy Brest. He thinks I'm dirt, and always did, ever since I was a little kid, chasing me and beatin' on me, saying I'm no good at all for the place he lives, and my family, too. He a colonel's son with plenty of money, and all the time new bikes and scooters he never let me ride, and goes to a school that costs tons, where all his friends think they're just better'n gold, their parents, too. He whupped me good more'n once before, though I'd be lyin' if I didn't say I fought back tooth and nail to let'm know just who he was fuckin' with.

I'm standing there and I start shakin', face all quivery, because I ain't never said nothing to nobody bad as what he says to me. But he goes on, saying awful things, even calling my sister a whore, which sure as hell ain't true, talking so much 's like he's crazy with it. He's tryin' to make me cry but I won't give it to'm, and 'cause of that he's lookin' madder'n hell.

Then suddenly — *wap!*

He chucks that basketball square in my face.

I fall down. Blood's coming out my nose and I feel

my face all wet with it. Hear his shoes scraping on the pavement coming toward me and I curl up.

Get up! he yells. Get up and fight!

I yelp out but that's all. My face hurts like crazy, nose is busted I think, though it ain't really, and I tuck my head down, knees up, so's if he starts kicking I'll maybe not get hit too bad. Through my knees I can just see his feet in them fancy sneakers he wears and I'm thinking maybe I fuckin' had enough when, God damn.

Damnedest thing happened.

Them fancy sneakers fly right up off the ground and a second later, me still looking through that space of my knees, I see his whole body come crashing down on the concrete 'bout eight foot from me, and he's looking like he sees monsters.

I sit up. Blood's everywhere on my face and shirt but I don't care, I'm too surprised. I see Jimmy Brest there on the ground, and another boy, a man, standing over him.

Richie Harrigan.

He's looking down at Brest, who don't move. Looking at Brest with this sort of mean look, animal look, lips pulled back, but his arm's out pointing at me.

What you call him! he says.

Then he pitches back a leg and drop-kicks Brest's ass.

What was it! You call him *trash?* What about *me,* fucker? You think *I'm* trash?

He kicks him again, and Brest sort'f scuffles back a bit.

Me, I pick trash, Richie says. Thumps his own chest with's fist saying that. You think *I'm* trash 'cause I pick it?

Richie kicks him again, not hard but sort of disgusted. Then he steps back a yard and I swear to God he spits right on'm.

My daddy got more money than your daddy, Richie says. You know that. I *bet* you do. C'mon. Get your ass up. You want to fight so bad, come on and fight *me.*

Brest don't move, just lies there moaning.

Richie shoves'm with's foot.

You call him trash again, I'll get you. You know I can. You *know* what I did to your brother. I *kicked* that pussy's ass.

Richie ain't tall as Brest but he's brawny, like I said. Got big muscles on his chest and arms. I know he whupped Brest's brother once, the one who later died in the war. Happened back when they was in school together, year they won the trophy with the big silver man on it. Richie, he looks like that trophy. Top-heavy, I mean. Everybody knows he can whup anybody.

He's going on about beating Brest's brother and I'll tell you, no matter how hurt I felt from what Brest said and how he hit my face, it's kind'f mean what Richie says, 'cause everybody remembers how Brest cried when his brother died, cried right out on the street. I mean, for a second there I was glad Richie come to help me, but now it was all just a nasty fuckin' mess, the sort of thing I hope you never see. 'Cause Richie says so much and scares him so much he starts to cry.

And Richie starts to laugh.

He looks at me. Looking at Brest, Richie's mouth was funny, lips pulled back tight over his teeth and his whole face savage like nothing I ever seen 'cept in some horror movie, but when he looks at me he shakes that off and smiles.

You gonna tell me if this fucker punk does it again?

I'll tell, I say. I gotta agree 'cause I sure don't want him mad at me. Fucker scares me, that's the goddamn truth.

You do that, he says, and kicks Brest again.

Then he comes over to me and takes my hand. C'mon, Monkey Boy, get up, let's leave this pile of shit.

He pulls me to my feet and we walk off, back around front where we talk a minute leaning on his truck, him smoking a cigarette and smiling at the trees, happy with what he done.

CHAPTER SEVEN

Back home I cleaned up some standing there over the sink, second floor bathroom, soap on my face. And after gettin' a lil' to eat I come in the living room, where I see my daddy sitting on that old ratty sofa we got crost the room from the old TV, which weren't even turned the hell on.

Hi, Daddy, I say.

Hi, son, he says. He kind'f leans up and scratches, then leans back. And that's all he does.

Leezie, she's over the side of the room near the hall where I come up, sort'f quiet but huffin' and puffin', her eyes all red with rage. She got a lot of makeup on'r face and I swear she looks like a sort'f angry, pretty clown.

Daddy says, Billy, next time you go out do me a favor, would you? Get some boxes.

What for? I say.

We gotta pack, he says. He's just staring at the dead TV set.

For what? I say.

We gotta move, he says.

Why don't you turn the TV on? I say.

He can't! Leezie screams. She's standing right next to me and she yells it right in my ear and I jump back.

Dang, girl! I says. You screamin' in my ear! Let up on me, will ya?

The TV's been turned off, she says.

I look around at the lights. What, the whole thing? They shut off the electric? How come the lights is on?

Just the cable shows, my daddy says, staring ahead.

I look over at the TV set. I can see us reflected, standing there in the green/gray screen.

God damn, I says.

Don't curse, Leezie says.

Scuze my language, I say.

I stand there a minute and I'm thinking.

Then I go on up to the TV. Stood there with my back turned.

I can't tell you how I felt. It was like the whole house was sitting on me, and nobody was doing nothing, and nobody was gonna even *try* to do anything. 'Cause you can see with what I'm telling you that nothing was comin' from Daddy or Leezie, 'cause all they wanted to do was mope and give up and get boxes and move out to God knows where, 'cause there weren't no place I knew we could go 'cept maybe the street, and that's one thing I ain't ever gonna do.

They all just waitin' on me, I thought. So I turned around and started.

Daddy, we ain't moving, I say.

What? he says. He jerks like I kicked him.

I said we ain't moving. Ain't losing the house. I won't have it.

What the hell are *you* going to do about it! Leezie shrilled.

Make money, I says. Like I promised you.

Ha!

She moves crost the room and sits next to Daddy. Then she looks at me.

You make any money today?!

A little, I said. Yesterday and today.

How much little?!

I figure, I got twelve for lawn mowing, Richie gave me five, and out with Marvin eleven more.

Right now, twenty-eight dollars, I say. But more's comin'.

That's nothing! she says.

49

Might pay the TV bill, I say. How much we get from Social Services?

I didn't say it before but there's a whole pile of mail on the table in front of Daddy. Something like thirty envelopes. Them people at Social Services, they love sending letters. They tell you how much you spent, how much you got, when it started, and when it all gonna end. Any little thing you do they send you a letter about, and if you don't keep up, they cancel all they giving you. You can see it on the computer if you got one, 'cause everything they put on paper they put there, too. But we ain't got one, a computer, I mean.

Wouldn't matter anyway. Daddy ain't opened none of the letters.

They want me to go to a meeting, he says. I missed it.

About what?

Job. Job counselor.

You going?

Missed it, he said again.

What? I said. He sort'f mumbled and I couldn't hear him.

He said he missed it! Leezie yells.

Quit yellin', I say, 'cause I'm just about sick of her razzin' me. And then I look at her good, sitting there next to Daddy on the sofa. She looks scared, sure, but there's something else, too. With all this yellin' and all that makeup on her face and'r eyes blazin' at me I start to wonder — *What's she up to?* Do she got something on'r mind? 'Cause she gets that way sometimes, all sneaky and full'f secrets she don't tell nobody till whatever it is 's all over and you can't do nothing about it. So I'm feelin' suspicious, 'cause Leezie's just 'bout the most stubborn girl you ever met, and once she's set on something you best not get in'r way.

But just what she was after right then I didn't know, 'cept it weren't about helpin' me make no money to save the house, that's for damn sure.

It's too far away to go, Daddy says. I took the bus but it was just too far. It got late. You need a car to get there.

He don't look good, Daddy. Short like me, and stocky, too, but all tired out. Gray. Gray all over. And when he moves he's stiff. He's only fifty-four, but he's done, I can tell it. Done with workin'. With living, almost. Worried me, seein' that. He needs help, I'm thinkin'. Got to get back on 's feet. But exactly what to do about it I couldn't say.

He can't ride the bus all day to get there, Leezie says. It's way out in the county.

God damn, I think. *Oh, God damn.*

All right, I say. Well how much we get?

Eight-fifty, Daddy says.

Cash? I say.

He nods.

We can't never live on that, I think. I seen enough rent posters in the neighborhood, and even worse neighborhoods when I'm out with Marvin.

Need at least twice that, I say.

How? Leezie says.

I look at her. She looks at Daddy, pats his gray arm. He's still looking at the dead TV set. Then they both look at me, waiting for answers, and I can't say nothing 'cause it's just me an' four eyes staring at me.

I'm going upstairs, I say.

Had me enough for a while.

I put ice on my nose and slept a few hours. When I got up it was dark outside. Dark inside, too. Red numbers on my lit-up clock said nine thirty. My nose still hurt and I was feeling a bit frazzed getting hit by Brest and thinking how now that Richie beat'm he really gonna be coming after my ass, which with everything else going on was just one thing too much. What Leezie said stung me hard, and I felt bad about it. I mean, there she goes one day getting me to promise, and the next day laughing in my face like it's something I can't do. But that'd been her way ever since our mother died, crying one minute and bossy the next.

And now she was wearin' all them skimpy clothes and that makeup, and going out nights to places I don't know where, with Daddy too sunk in hisself to stop'r, and me just wonderin' what's she set on.

But even more than that I was thinking 'bout that house next to Simon Hooper's, and what was in those boxes lying on the floor in there, and if there was other stuff I might find if I went inside to look.

And it weren't easy, thinking that.

The truth is, more happened between me and my mother than just what I said to Marvin. One night close to when she died, she took my hand and pleaded for me to swear to the Lord I wouldn't do another thing like that, so's there wouldn't be no more stains on my soul like them nuns at school say, and so's she could go to her rest without worrying about me so much. And I went ahead and swore like she wanted. And that made thinking 'bout going in that house real hard.

But I gotta say the idea'd come to me that to save our house I might just have to do exactly what I swore I wouldn't. What would my mother say to that? What if I *got* to slip to help Daddy and Leezie?

Thinking like that, my mind sort'f made itself up, and I thought, *Tonight,* 'cause I couldn't see no other way. And bad as it sounds I gotta say the old thrill came back, and I felt the hair on my arms risin', just thinking of what I might find.

Few minutes later I went down. Daddy was still there, sitting on the sofa in the dark. Leezie, she was upstairs.

I don't say nothing, but Daddy says, Billy?

I'm headed to the door and stop.

Yeah, Daddy?

Know what I seen today? he says. I was going to that job counselor. It got too late, so I got off the bus. Went to this shop I saw. I stood out there an hour looking at that shop. FRESH FISH, it says on the sign, and the name of the man who owns it. Wish I had that.

He turns his face to me, just enough light from the streetlights outside come in the window to shine rings off his glasses. Can you imagine that, Billy? he says, sort'f whispers. It'd take care'f us all. And you could work with me.

I smile. *He's just dreamin'*, I think.

Fish? I say.

No, not that. He looks down, then up again, slow. *Fruit,* he says. What your mother loved. Remember how she used to set a bowl out every day?

Yeah, I remember, I said.

He nodded. That's what. FRESH FRUIT, right there on the sign. Can't you see that? Right on the sign with my name on it. And your name on it.

He sat up a bit. Looked at me.

Well, maybe it ain't just a dream, I'm thinkin'. 'Cause for a second there he had more life in'm than he had all day, and even smiled a little.

Then he slunk back on the sofa in the dark.

All right, Daddy, all right, I say, and I opened the door. Then I turned and put the money I made on the sofa beside him.

You pay the TV cable, I say.

He don't budge.

Then I go.

CHAPTER EIGHT

I went up the alley behind the houses so's not to get seen, and after a while I sat and waited until I seen most house lights go out and I figured it was past eleven. Then I went on, and after a few minutes was out back Simon Hooper's. I listened to hear if Bear was out, 'cause if he is you can hear'm pawing the ground or his collar jangling, and it'd be no good for him to sniff me out and start barking and tryin' to get at me. But everything was quiet. So a minute later I was climbing over that board fence into the yard of the house next door.

No lights was on at the house. There was trees all round, and bushes, all of'm overgrown, so going up on the porches was no trouble, but the doors'n windows were locked. I'd figured on that. So I went around side, where the yard was narrow near the board fence. I chinned up to the window I'd looked in earlier, and tried to shove it open, but it was locked tight. Then I tried a few more windows, all round the house, and none of'm budged an inch. So I looked up at the shadows of the trees. One had a branch overhanging the second floor roof, so I climbed up and dropped down.

I crawled over the roof till I found a window I could open, and real quiet I got to work. I couldn't see inside 'cause behind the window, it was hung with black plastic, kind you get from a big trash bag, sort you might use for bagging up leaves you raked. I figured it was there 'cause either the folks who owned it didn't want nobody looking inside or else they'd sprayed for bugs and didn't want to let no air in.

After a minute I wiggled open the window and slid it up, didn't even squeak. Then I put a leg in and ducked inside, tearing away the plastic as I moved. I stepped down real soft, no noise at all, and I went on.

I gone through three/four rooms, stopping every couple feet to listen, but never heard a thing. Couldn't see nothing. Every window in there was covered with that black plastic. House was empty. Somebody'd been around, sure, 'cause here and there I walked over trash and cans I felt crush under my feet, beer cans, and I smelled old stale cigarettes and reefers'n such. Whole place stunk bad with never getting aired, lemme tell you.

Ever once in a while wind would move through the rooms and them bags on the windows would sort'f puff out, I mean inflate a little, and it spooked me, seeming like the whole house was breathing.

I come downstairs'n went around and saw the kitchen. In there on the stove was a frying pan. Somebody'd had a bite to eat, I could see that, because the pan weren't washed but dirty with grease, prob'ly just warmed some takeout. A little clock dial on the stove was lit and that was the only electric I seen on in there. Course I never tried no light switches.

Next I come in the room I'd looked in when I was at Hooper's. Like I said, the plastic on the window there had come away one side where it was stapled, and that let a little light in, just the faintest.

First thing I done was check out the clothes I seen earlier. What I found was a dark flannel thing, more like a shirt than a coat, same sort lumberjacks wear. I stooped and grabbed it. Close to my face I could just see it was green plaid, with black boxy lines on it. Nothing in the pockets, so I tossed it down. There was a few other coats lying there too, prob'ly put in here for summer storage. I picked one up.

That flannel shirt was sized for a man, but this coat

was a boy's and would'f fit me if I'd tried it. I held it out and seen it was a winter coat, one'f them puffy ones all filled with feathers some boys wear, with a pair of mittens fixed to the sleeve. I felt around'n unclipped some sort of buckle, and they came loose. So's not to drop'm I stuffed'm in my back pocket, mittens, I mean. Pockets was empty on the coat, and I was gonna toss it but I seen something wrote on the collar and I was curious. I wished I had me some sort'f light, 'cause I could see it was initials, wrote in Magic Marker, way a boy's mother writes when she don't want him to lose his coat at school. But try all I could, I couldn't make them letters out, 'cause they was too faded.

And then I just shook my head, thinking what a dumbass I was to'f busted in a house to find something worth taking and now was trying to read letters on some boy's coat, so I tossed't to the floor, disgusted.

Now I seen them boxes. I opened one of'm, and what I found first was just junk. I don't mean trash, but just stuff like can openers and cups and saucers, sort'f things you might use if you was maybe camping out in a house but not really living there.

I closed it good so nobody'd know it been touched, and I went ahead and opened the next one, just to see. It was the same. Old cups and plates and knives and forks, and I cussed under my breath at the luck of it.

I was gonna give up when my finger went under a lip of cardboard and I lifted it. It was there making the box have two layers, a top one with the cups and such on it, and another underneath. I didn't want to pull it up and knock all the cups out 'cause'f the noise, so what I done was just feel around, and my little finger caught on something sharp, so I pulled it up and out.

It came up slow, 'cause it was snagged on other stuff down there. But when I got it out I held it close to my face, and even in the dimmest light I seen it was a necklace stuck with hard little jewels.

I didn't say nothing out loud. But inside my voice was whooping. What I done next was stoop down, and real careful not to make no noise I pulled up the rest of that cardboard piece, all the cups on top sliding over.

I couldn't see it all, but it was full, and I dug my hand in it, pulling stuff out to feel what it was. There were rings, and a sort'f crown piece just for the front of the head I seen girls wear when they dressed as princesses on Halloween. There was more necklaces, and then these fancy gloves, long ones that go way up to your elbow. And under it all was this ladies' dress, or two or three of'm, I didn't take'm out, acting like a pillow so what's on top don't get all scratched.

I closed the box just like it'd been, and I crouched there thinking 'bout the best way to get it out. I couldn't get it down that tree in the dark, damn thing was heavy. But really I was thinking I ain't just found forty-eight thousand, but maybe even more, if all these jewels turned out to be real.

Then the door opened in front of the house and I froze dead still.

Usually in a house I look first to find hiding places, places to sneak to if I can't get out quick and know somebody might come looking to see who's there. But I hadn't done it 'cause I'd thought nobody'd ever come around, and because it was so dark I didn't remember nothing of where I'd been, so I had nowhere to run to.

Coming into that room I'd shut the door behind me. I couldn't open it now and run out 'cause'f the noise it would make. So what I done was step back maybe a yard, one big swooping step, to where I'd be behind the door if it opened. And all the while I was hearing somebody walking through the house, and damn near shitting bricks as I heard.

The footsteps stopped awhile and I heard a toilet flush, and then they come on again, footsteps, coming toward me. I was praying to God they might turn away, but the door opened then, pulling air in the room and puffing out them window bags, and me right there behind the door.

Whoever it was just come in the room and stood there. I couldn't see hardly nothing, and whoever it was didn't move. There I heard some shuffling around and some light come on 'cause this man—I could see past the door enough to know it was a man—had a flashlight.

Flashlight was that new kind that only shines where you point it, else he'd put some sort'f sleeve on the front to narrow the beam. It didn't light the whole room, but just where he aimed it, down on the floor at the coats. When he'd come in I opened my mouth big, 'cause if you do that you can breathe silent, but I don't think I breathed at all. I just stood there, three feet behind him, and it was like a crazy dream where you can't get out, and he was shuffling his hand on the coats on the floor just where I'd dropped'm. Then he laid down his light and piled'm all in his arms.

All I could think was, *If he turns, I'm caught.*

Course, I didn't know then who this fucker was, and that if he turned I was dead.

But he didn't turn, just flicked off the flashlight and put it away somewhere. Then he dumped them coats on top of that box, same one with the jewels in it, picked it all up with a heave, turned out the door and shut it.

I didn't breathe yet, and I waited a good long time till after I heard that front door shut and a car drive off 'fore I moved at all. Then I felt my pants leg and laughed, 'cause I'd pissed myself and not even known it.

I went upstairs, though it scared me to death to do

it, and went along to the room where I found the open window, and I went out onto the roof, quiet as anything, putting the plastic back up on them bent staples just like I'd found it, and closing that window just so.

I come down the tree, went over the board fence, and come out Simon Hooper's yard. Dodged through other yards, still so scared I could barely think to myself, and sometimes stayed in black shadows four/five minutes, just to be sure nobody saw.

Took me an hour to get home, I moved so slow, and when I was finally back in my room I stood there breathing hard, still scared as shit.

Then I felt round my back pocket and laughed out loud. I still had them mittens with me, and I pulled'm out'n threw'm crost the room, laughing at how dumb I was, going in a house and finding all them jewels, and coming out with just a pair of old mittens.

CHAPTER NINE

I dreamed all night about being in that house and that dark clump of a man crouched down just a yard from me, him on his knees and them jewels in 's hands shining through even though there weren't no light. Gave me the horrors like I never known. Marvin was right to worry 'bout me slippin', and that's what I'd done, slipped so bad I almost got caught, which with everything else going on right then really would have done me. 'Cause if I'd got caught, who gonna make the forty-eight thousand?

So the next few weeks I mowed lawns every day just to keep my ass out'f trouble. Some days I went out on jobs with Richie Harrigan, hauling things, and I also went around with a boy I know, Sam Tate, who got a paper route and don't mind if I take over for him now and again.

Every day I was at houses asking for work, 'specially old houses and beat-up ones, and ones that ain't never been cleaned or cleared, so's when I come to the door I could say to who answered just what work I could do for'm. And what with also making deliveries with Marvin and driving round with Richie, I was all over the neighborhood, seeing every house around, more than any cop or even one'f them government agents they said was going door to door. But I weren't making nobody nervous askin' questions 'bout Tommy Evans and Tuckie Brenner, and getting'm all on edge like maybe they was suspected, 'cause I ain't no cop, that's for damn sure. I was just asking for work, but doing that every day I saw hundreds of houses, and also peeked around sly when nobody was looking, trying to see if there was anything extra around I might grab if the time was right, you get me?

Another thing I done was keep my eye out where stores was, 'specially when I was out near downtown with Richie. I was lookin' for places that might be good for settin' up my daddy's fruit stand, hopin' if I could find a place good and cheap Daddy'd get excited and maybe start to plan it for real.

But this all come to something else, too. 'Cause later on, when I really started trying to find out who took them boys, I thought about all them weeks I'd spent looking for work, and things that didn't mean much then started risin' up different and darker than I'd known when I first seen'm.

Lookin' for work was harder than you might think, 'cause a lot of them folks I asked thought I was foolin', me being the same boy who maybe they caught a year back soapin' their car or chuckin' eggs, or thought maybe I'd lifted something off their porch or outta their garage, which sometimes was true and sometimes not. But I went ahead and asked all the same, 'cause I needed that money and didn't care how embarrassed I got. Felt good keeping busy, some days going at it twelve hours, not stopping till I was fall-down tired. I didn't think nothing 'bout what I seen that night in the dark house, days went by and it all slipped my mind, till even the scare went away.

Then come a day when it all came back to me, even stranger than it was before.

One house I knew needed work was the big old place down Church Lane, that dead end off Denton Avenue, and I went over there thinking that house ain't had its gutters cleaned for years 'cause the lady living there never went out the house and had Marvin bring her drugs and groceries, both.

End of Church Lane is where the woods begin and there's that big hill behind the house all covered with scraggly bushes and busted trees like after a storm. House is the one that's all gray, with them towers coming off the roof shaped like cones, and they're black, and the shingles ain't just flat and square but shaped in little round chips and sort of pretty, and the whole house would be pretty too and like something in a carnival at the beach if it was painted bright, but right now looks like nothing but a big old dead birthday cake, turned all black and gray.

I knocked and she come to the screen, the old lady, all skinny as sticks and wearing sharp-shaped glasses under her scraggly old hair, it all in a bunch. After she got over being just scared of seeing me through the screen she gave in, mainly 'cause I warned'r how if she don't clean'm now, gutters, I mean, the whole house gonna fall apart and be full of workers from the city who gonna put her out after crawling all around her house and spoiling her privacy.

She looked hard at me, her eyes squinty behind her glasses, and her mouth all pinched up. Then she said, No, son. I don't want any help from you. Now you go *away!* Her voice sounded all shrill like some nasty bird.

But I weren't hearing that, so I said, You gonna get an injunction from the city, ma'am. Neighbors round here'll do it, and you gonna have cops all round and men stamping through your living room tearing it all apart, and then they gonna take the whole place and sell it out from under you and putchu in the old folks' home, I *know* it.

I sold it hard, making like I might put in the injunction *myself* if she don't hire me, and you should'f seen her eyes go wide, 'specially with me talking so much 'bout the old folks' home.

She agreed to twenty dollars, whole job.

Now, she a crazy lady and wouldn't let me inside her house at all. So I went up the side, climbing first the porch posts and then doing this sort of jump-flip to get on the roof, and then damn near kicking myself seeing I could'f got up easier and safer just climbing one of them pine trees beside her house and jumping down.

First level roof I cleared, using a bag, plastic one she handed to me out a shuttered window. I pulled ten years' worth of twigs and leaves and pine cones out the gutters and stuffed'm in the bag, and when it was full I dropped it down to the yard. Roof shingles was old and cracked and covered with dirt and bird dookie, and some of'm busted under my tread making me slip, but I never did tell her.

Next roof up I did use the pine tree to get there, tallest one. But for way up on top at the attic, the pinnacle up there where it's round and got them diamond windows, I had to climb with my fingertips and shoe sides, and I tell you it was scary, half the time hanging all teeter-totter over the open space'f the lower roofs with nothing to hold on to but an old shutter clasp.

Up there I filled bags and tossed'm down, holding'm in my teeth as they got all filled up. Near the windows I peeked inside, and what I saw was just dark clutter with blankets and dust and old brown wood, and stuff like framed pictures on the walls and right there in the middle of the floor a sort of woman-dummy like you see in department stores, just like a ghost standing in the murk, but with no head, and swathes of cloth hanging off'r from a dress that never got made. It was hard to see more, 'cause that diamond window glass was thick and warpy and inside the room was old and dark.

Then I seen something else.

First I could barely make it out, and it was just a feeling. But then something strange hit me and I looked hard.

Right there inside was a few boxes, cardboard ones stacked on the wall. And my mouth went dry.

'Cause I be damned if they ain't the same boxes I seen in the dark house next to Simon Hooper's, boxes with tomatoes printed on the sides.

I hung on there thinking. I was damn curious. Maybe

there *was* something worth getting in those boxes. Maybe those jewels *was* real. I seen'm in one house, and now I seen'm here, so somebody was taking care just what to do with'm. I figured the old lady downstairs maybe had done it. But it was a *man* who come in that house, and there weren't ever no man around here. So unless she'd hired a man, I couldn't say what happened. And then I think, *Who's the man to be going in that dark house,* and *coming in here?*

For a second I thought I might ask'r, 'bout both the man and the boxes. But then I figured it be better if I just had a look myself, 'cause why tell'r them boxes interested me at all? I mean have a look right then and there, with the old lady downstairs and nobody else around to see me. Yeah, after that night next to Hooper's I'd sort'f sworn off bustin' in houses. But I weren't worried about that right now 'cause who was there to catch me? Just a little old lady, and if she caught me I'd just say some lie.

So I tried.

But them windows were tight, I tell you, all painted shut, and the glass had that church wire in it, heavy lead stuff you'd need a brick to break.

So I figured I'd have me a look later on. Just had to think the best way and time, and I'd be on it.

Hour later I was back down on the porch and had my

twenty bucks and Miss Gurpy, that's the old lady's name, reached out and pinched my cheek to be nice, though it hurt me, and handed me a kind of sandwich through the gap in the old screen door, but walking away I tossed it 'cause to tell it true, it didn't smell too fresh.

CHAPTER TEN

So there I was walking home, going down the street at curfew all ready to go cutting over yards when a car stops behind me and I hear a voice that says, *Hey, Zeets,* and I turn around.

I can't hardly see who's driving 'cause the car's all full of smoke, reefer smoke I smell ten foot off, but I know the car. 'S one of them old Fords you see around, sort of car that ain't a sedan but looks like one on the front end, 'cept it got a pickup truck bed behind, called a Ranchero. Old car, blue paint all faded and the old chrome speckled with rust.

Boy who called out to me is Skugger, neighborhood kid actually named Ryan Skuggs, but his friends, they call him Skugger for no reason I could understand, 'cause who the hell would want to be called that? But that's their way, them rich boys. They got all them names, Tuckie and Skugger and Topher, and go round calling out to each other like they talking in a code, and wear the same sort of clothes their mothers buy'm, like them puffy jackets, and do all the same things, too, like they all in a club just for themselves with nobody else allowed, thank you.

Anyway, Skugger, he's sittin' there on the passenger side with his head out the window. Hey, Zeets, he says, kind'f smiling at me, you wanna buy some weed? I've got some good shit, man, he says.

I shake my head for no. Ain't interested, I say, and I walk the other way. 'Cause this here Skugger is a boy who sells drugs to all the boys around, pot and pills mostly but worse stuff too, and he been caught at it plenty of times. Used to go to that private school with all them other boys once, but since gettin' caught the last time, got kicked out. One thing I'll say is he makes good money at it. But I never done no drugs and don't care to sell'm, neither. And right now I figure the last thing I need is to get caught with pills in my pocket by some cop.

He keeps leaning his chin on the doorjamb there on the car, watching me, window rolled down, and he says, You better look out, Zeets. Better watch your ass.

I give him a stare.

Why's that? I ask.

Jimmy Brest told me he's looking for you.

Now ole Skugger grins, sort'f nasty, like he's onto something, like the secret is told.

Let'm look, I say. *Here* I am. Ain't afraid of'm.

This time is gonna be different, Skugger says.

Yeah, I says. 'Cause it'll go the other way.

He just laughs. Opens his mouth a big O for a big *Ha-ha*, though he ain't really laughing.

Look out for yourself, he says, sort'f friendly, and he turns and settles back in his seat puffing the last of some smoke out his mouth and pulling down over his head this hat he got on, knit hat that hangs off 's head like a two-foot sock even though it's summertime. Then the car slides forward, but at the last second with his hand still on the doorjamb, Skugger, he gives me one of them fuck-you fingers as he goes away.

I cussed him good right then, you bet I did, screaming, Goddamn motherfucker kiss my ass, scuze my language. And the car, it jerked to a stop, tires screeched, like he's gonna maybe get on out and do something about it. But do that fucker come back for me? Shit no. He didn't want a busted lip that day.

I still got a few blocks to cover, so I go through a yard and over a porch where there ain't nothing but empty chairs and quiet toys and dust. Then I dodge down into an alley and go on walking slow over the concrete, garages on both sides.

Then something funny come to me.

When Skugger'd talked I'd watched that man in there driving the car, this sort'f hairy-looking man about Richie Harrigan's age, 'cause I'd seen him round a few times over the years, last few years, and he and Skugger was always driving around together, as was lots of other boys who hung out with'm and liked to party. And even though I ain't never met the man driving, right then I felt there was something real familiar about him, but I couldn't say just what 'cause of all that smoke blowin' round inside the car.

Then just like that I hear feet running up behind me. I turned back quick and saw Jimmy Brest, tall and straight and coming fast.

ZEETS! he yelled, his face looking on fire.

I didn't stay to hear more.

I ran.

I went through a gate into a yard, and knowing Brest was fast on his feet, I dodged right through the walk-in door on the side of a garage. I ducked just in time to see'm run past, the motherfucker running along with a big bag of chips in his hand, and his voice sounding funny yelling 'cause his mouth's all full of chips.

I figured I had maybe thirty seconds till he backtracked. I stood still a second to slow my breath and listen. I wondered how the hell he'd found me, what with me just getting warned like I did. Then the thought come to me that Skugger'd prob'ly got pissed when I cussed him, called the fucker'n told him where I was.

The big garage door was open, so I went straight back out in the alley. I heard Brest off in some yard yelling, *Where are you, fucker?* but I didn't hang around.

Across the alley was another garage, and I went in. Was the sort with a stairs to the rafters, wood stairs you get down by pulling on a rope, and I pulled. Keeping the rope in my hand I yanked the stairs back up once I got on the rafters, and just in time, too. Because a second later Brest came in below. I was sitting in the dark on a rafter and I heard'm, knocking things around, saying, *Where the fuck are you?* And me, I'm thinking, *I hope the fucker starts up after me, 'cause there some paint cans up'ere gonna make friends with his head if he do,* and I almost bust out laughin' thinking that, the dumb fucker. But a second later he was out in the alley, running until his footscrapes faded away.

CHAPTER ELEVEN

When I got home it was after curfew. Sun was throwing
shadows of trees all 'long the street. Leezie was there
standing on the porch, house all dark behind her.

Where's Daddy?

Took a bus ride, she says. Out all day.

Job counselor?

Don't know, she said.

I looked at her. She was wearing this pair of pants
cut so short the pockets flapped out, and she had this sort
of pearly paint on her toenails, red it was, and for a shirt
she had the flimsiest thing, no different than being naked,
looking through it you could see her whole shape, and that
black strappy underwear she got on underneath't. Her face
was made up too. Blue on the eyes right up to under the

eyebrows, brown stuff on her cheeks like dark hollows, and mouth so red it looked like she'd split her lip. Wearin' perfume too. Shit, I could smell'r ten foot off.

Leezie, why you dressed like that? I said.

She looked at me and winced. I ain't dressed, she said. I'm *getting* dressed. Still ain't put my shoes on!

Do you know what some boys say about you?

I don't care. It ain't true.

I know that, I said. I know it. But you stand there all day looking like that, it won't matter. People gonna think it's true anyway. So why not dress regular? Why not go put a dress on like you used to and wash your face. Will you do it?

Billy? she said.

Yar? I said.

Go to fuckin' hell, she says. Then she turns around and goes inside, screen door smackin' shut behind her.

I went up my room. Was tired from all day working, but that didn't matter, and when I lay down I could think of nothing but what the hell was going on with the coat and the house and the boxes, and who that damn man was who come in the room, who also got full rights to go in Miss Gurpy's, if them boxes tell it right.

I rolled over and was just about to shut my eyes when I stopped.

Saw them mittens on the floor where I threw'm.

I laughed, thinking 'bout how they could be jewels instead of mittens if I'd been smart enough.

But I got an idea. Maybe these mittens *is* worth something, but I just don't know what. So I sat up and reached over and took'm in my hands. I looked at'm for a while, a good five minutes, turning'm this way and that. I'm thinkin' maybe I got'm, took'm, for a reason, and I sit there trying to figure it out.

But I can't. Too damn tired, for one thing.

Then I hear something. A car. Out front. Big engine sound like a truck revving, just faster, and a radio real loud with some singer screeching like he's falling off a cliff.

Now like I said, Leezie'd been going out most nights, and never saying who with. Made me real curious, her doing that, 'specially how she weren't payin' no mind at all to the curfew. I thought findin' out just where she's goin' and who with might sort'f clue me in to what she's up to, 'cause she ain't a girl to say what she's gonna do but just goes 'head and does it.

So I jumped up fast and run downstairs and when I come in the hall I find Leezie standing there, ready to go out.

Who's here? I say.

'S my date, Leezie says.

I dodge out front to the porch and look. Car's down there parked in the street, a big GTO, old car but all souped up, painted slate gray with a six on the side, in red. Has an engine scoop stickin' up through the hood and back tires wider than truck tires but with no tread, slicks is what they called.

Sitting in it is a boy I know who got this long frizzy hair, yellow, and arms folded to show off his muscles, tattoos all over the goddamn place.

Leezie comes out.

You going out with *him?* I say.

Why not! she says.

That's Bad-Ass Ricky!

His *name* is Ricky Morgan, Leezie says, like I don't know.

Leezie, you can't go out with him! He's the worst boy around! He tried to get me to rob Shatze's once! I seen him in the back of squad cars plenty of times!

Go to hell, Billy, she says. I like him! He treats me real nice! He's taking me to the circus!

She's trying to sound bold, but I can tell she's embarrassed a little.

I say, Don't do it, Leezie! He don't respect girls. Tell him to go away.

She glares at me, her face so colored it looks wild.

He talks dirty 'bout'm, I said.

She goes to smack me and I duck.

Ain't lying! I say.

Down there Ricky, he come out the car and is leaning against it, not coming up 'cause the damn fool's stopped in the middle of the street. Leezie, she goes down, walking in that gonna-fall stilt-walk girls got walking in them spike shoes. And she goes up and the bastard puts his arm around her.

Hiya, Ricky! I say. I'm tryin' to sound friendly 'cause I seen this bastard get violent, beat the shit outta plenty of boys for no damn reason at all, and I sure don't want him mad at me.

He don't answer but just raises his hand and squints and makes like a pistol with his fingers and fires, and then laughs, the fucker. Wearin' an Iron Maiden T-shirt, know the kind I mean? Me, I laugh too just to look agreeable, but boy I feel bad for Leezie. And before I even get back inside the door he's got her in the car and then slipped through his window hisself not even opening his door and *BOOM* that GTO is five hundred yards up the street.

Circus my ass, I think.

I turn to go back in, but I stop, looking down.

I still got them mittens in my hand.

CHAPTER TWELVE

I sat in the kitchen and ate a little and when Daddy got home I talked to him 'bout what he'd done all day, which was nothing, 'cept he gone to see that man who owns the fish shop and talked with'm all about what it takes to run a store like that, what sort'f papers you gotta draw up and how much stake you need to have a go.

It was good hearin' he really went so far as to actually meet the man and ask questions like he done, and I wanted to tell'm 'bout how I'd been goin' around writin' down addresses of empty stores I seen, but I figured it be best to wait till I called a few and found out just how much rent money they'd all want before getting Daddy's hopes up.

Daddy, he also found out you gotta have a truck to haul your stock up from them wholesalers downtown, and other things to boot you gotta own to get goin', like 'frigerators to keep it all cold.

He was pretty excited when he first started telling me, but after a while it seemed like there was so much to do and so much money needed for it that he got quiet and just sat there at the table. I told him it ain't all that hard and not to worry 'cause I'd help'm, but he just sort'f shook his head and didn't say nothing more, and I went upstairs.

But I didn't sleep.

My head was all full of thoughts, especially thoughts about when to go to Miss Gurpy's to check out them boxes, and really wishing she'd just let me clean her house on the inside, so I could take a look without no risk of sneaking in, and I figured I'd talk to Richie Harrigan about that.

One thing I gotta say is when I thought about the man or the house or the boxes, I didn't think 'bout what Leezie was doing out with Bad-Ass or worry 'bout Daddy moping downstairs—all that just slipped my mind. Ain't that funny? It was the best damn way I'd had to get my mind off things since I used to go out late nights ridin' on that old bike. 'Cept this time it was even better. 'Cause it was like a puzzle, with the only rule book the one I figure out myself, and nagging at me hard enough to make my worries just fade away.

So I'm lying there in bed like that, sort'f dreaming

almost about them boxes and the jewels and what to do to see'm, when just then I remember something and sit up straight like I been bit.

Remember how today Skugger'd warned me when he was in a car with a man? That's what I was thinking about now. At the time there'd seemed something familiar about that man. I don't mean who he was, 'cause even though I'd never met him and didn't know his name I'd seen him around time and again, always driving that same old car, and always with one boy or another who liked to get high.

But right then in bed I knew what it was that I'd seen.

It was his *coat,* or really the shirt he had on.

I remember I was looking at'm through the smoke in the car, and he was smoking a jay and so high he was sort'f poking it at his face and missing his mouth, and sparks was falling on his shirt and he was rubbing'm out. And I saw it was a *green* shirt, green plaid, same as lumberjacks wear.

It was the goddamn shirt I'd seen on the floor of the dark house, lying there with the puffy jacket. Shirt looked hot for the weather and his face was all sweaty but he was smokin' so much reefer it didn't seem to faze'm.

I lay there staring, thinking 'bout that and all the other things I'd seen, and tryin' my damndest to find a way to put'm together. And I must say it pissed me off not knowing just how to do it.

Then suddenly I thought, *I want to see that man* . . .

Meaning I want to spy on him, follow him around, see what the hell he's up to.

I was out of bed in a second and out the window even faster, climbing down the fire escape and walking crost the yard to the alley.

Th'night was dark and it was just a few minutes before I come near Simon Hooper's. I'd run all the way and got short of breath and doubled up awhile panting, then when I was ready I went through Hooper's yard and over the board fence to the house next door. I was in the front yard and nothing had changed. Porch was empty. No lights anywheres. And no sound, neither.

I went alongside and the window I'd looked in was covered now, same as the others, with black plastic, piece of a tarp, or just a trash bag. I felt a little bad 'cause I was hoping to see something, but there was nothing.

Then I went around back and stopped dead.

A car was parked there on the grass of the yard. Same car I'd seen Skugger in, blue Ranchero.

I went up to it. Tried the doors but they was locked. Looked inside, and I seen this man don't never clean his car, 'cause there a big mess of trash and cans on the floor, and on top it all Skugger's goofball hat, long one with the pompom at the end.

I was thinking to leave but I stopped.

A car's here, I thought. *So a man's here too.*

I looked around a sec, and then I went over to the board fence. Here, out back, there's a big old gnarled tree in that fence, I mean the fence comes up to both sides of it with the tree right in the middle. And nailed on the tree is these wood steps, pieces of two-by-four sawed about a foot wide nailed up by some boy who lived here long ago. I tried'm and they held tight, so I climbed.

When I was up in the tree with the leaves all round me I found the tree fort. I'd seen it before in daytime, just an old rotty thing of worn planks, and I'd never thought to go up it till now. What I did was climb on and spread myself out facedown, over a place where the planks was busted, looking down at the car in the yard.

I felt cold up there, wind was blowing over me. I don't know how long it took. Hour, maybe. But soon after that I heard a lock turning there on the back porch, and the door opened.

A man come out. But he didn't turn the light on. Not the house light in the room he was coming from, or the porch light outside. He stood for a minute, looking around, then he closed the door real quiet and come down the back porch steps and went to the fence, walking slow. At the fence he unlocked a lock, gave a shove, and the whole middle of the fence swung open into the alley behind. Then he got in the car and started it, but he didn't turn the lights on. He backed out real slow, and when he was in the alley he got out and closed the gate and then got back in the car and drove away, driving up the alley and never turning his lights on far as I could see.

I stayed in that tree ten more minutes, long enough to know he weren't coming right back.

I hadn't seen him good. Couldn't say who he was. Was too damn dark. Must be the same man who come in the room that night, but I couldn't tell for sure, 'cause down there in the yard with no lights on I'd only seen the shape of'm. From how he walked he was all thick and dumpy. Big, too.

Was it the man in the car today?

Maybe.

If he was, and knowing who Skugger was, I figured he's the man who gets'm the drugs, all that pot and them pills Skugger sells to his friends.

But why's he sneaking around in there, not turning on the lights?

I'm still looking at the house.

What's he hiding *in there?* I'm thinkin'.

I was getting close to something, and the closer I got, the more my other worries went away. *What is it? What is it?* Questions burned in my head. And right then they burned so hot I think I'd'f give all the money I made that summer just to know.

CHAPTER THIRTEEN

I couldn't think about it too much 'cause the next day they
turned the electric off and Daddy and me went downtown
real early. We had to go downtown 'cause we couldn't call
nobody 'cause the phone'd been turned off about a week
then and we had to go in person, to the electric company, I
mean, so's to get on what they call the low-income rate for
electrical consumption. Actually we could'f called 'cause
Leezie still got'r cell phone and don't ask me how she was
paying for it, prob'ly just sweet-talking some cell phone
operator, 'cause she never did get a job back then, just me.
But what I'm saying is she weren't home that morning,
she'd been out all night, and after seeing who she was going
out with I didn't even want to think about it.

Downtown after we got off the bus we went to

the building and waited in a long line just to get inside, then waited in another line, and they put Daddy on the runaround, always going to the wrong room and talking to the wrong person, till we got what they call an emergency reconnect 'cause there's children in the house, then got sent out 'cause Daddy, he ain't brought the right papers to prove lack of income, so they called it, so except for that emergency reconnect the whole thing was a goddamn waste of time.

But coming home before we got the bus — we got free tokens by the way, Welfare tokens — Daddy, he remembered the larder was open, Social Services Larder, they call it, sort of like a ugly grocery store, more like a cage with food in it. So we went there first, and filled the two bags they give you, we going up to these racks where they got macaroni and cheese mix and corn cereal and these packs of cottage cheese that Leezie likes and cans of red salmon I personally can't fuckin' stand.

So it weren't all a waste, the day, I mean, 'cause we got all that and lugged it home, which was hard work, 'specially seein' as how the bus stop up our way is at least half a mile from my house, and when we get there Leezie *still* ain't home and I'm thinking, *What's that bastard Bad-Ass Ricky doing with'r?*

Now I'd promised Marvin I'd go out early but I was late and I felt bad for it, 'specially thinkin 'bout the money

I could'f made. So after I got home I run down there. He was still out going his rounds, Miss Norris told me, so all I did was step out to the parking lot alongside and sit there, my back against the wall, my ass on the ground, feeling a shitload of gravel through my pants, chucking bits of that gravel at a sheared-off pipe I seen to see how many I could get in.

After about twenty minutes Marvin drove up.

He parked at the curb but then when he seen me he pulled in the lot and stopped right acrost from me. I'd been sitting there awhile and maybe I was worried about Leezie or thinking 'bout seeing that man last night, but Marvin looked at me like there was something wrong with my face, like I felt *terrible,* I mean, and he said, So, Billy, I guess you heard.

Now I did feel bad. Sort'f dreadful. I just looked at him and groaned, Oh God, Marvin, *now* what?

He looked a little surprised.

You don't know?

He didn't say nothing more, just reached aside. And when his hand come back up he was holding a piece of paper with Jimmy Brest's face printed on it, under where big black letters wrote *M-I-S-S-I-N-G.*

We drove and I was staring forward, looking at this piece of dashboard where the vinyl was cracked and had yellow foam in it, all tore up and brown at the edges under the crack. We'd go a block, stop, I'd jump out and tape a flyer, get back in, go another block, jump back out. That's how it went. We didn't talk at all, me and Marvin.

The street was bright, with the green of the trees all spread over it, and flashes of sunlight comin' through the leaves. The houses looked empty and clean and white under the gray roofs, set back far on the wide green lawns, no lawn furniture 'cause it ain't allowed around here, not on front lawns, no jungle gyms, neither, or kiddie pools, nothing to play on, just grass and flowers and ivy and trees everywhere thick as you please.

We got stopped three times. First by people in their yards who came over and talked about Jimmy Brest and the last time they seen him and where. Word was generally that he must still be around, that even if he was captured and kidnapped by this killer he had to still be in the neighborhood or in town at least, because here's where Tommy Evans was found. So even though there was this sense of him being already dead, there was the idea that maybe he'd be found, or the man who took him would. Day was sunny and I remember 'specially how when we talked the people was always in the sun, holding hands up to cover their eyes but it weren't any good, and they were squinting like they hurt, their eyes, I mean, and the streets and houses all seemed empty in rows behind'm.

Third time we was stopped it was a cop. He asked Marvin what he was doing with me, and we both told'm no Marvin ain't doing nothing wrong and we knowed each other real good and was even the ones hanging the flyers for Jimmy Brest and showed'm a bunch of'm. But this cop was young and dumb and new and looking for something to do, so he radioed in and wouldn't let us go until another cop showed up, officer named Dryker, big old cop with white hair, who knowed both Marvin and me, Marvin from just around and me from when he caught me once taking eggs off porches.

We talked and he asked us both if we knowed Brest and when we last seen him. I told him I did know him but hadn't seen him awhile, and Marvin said pretty much the same. Then looking at me, Dryker said what a wiseass I thought I was but that this man out there was killing boys and for me to mind the curfew, which was now an hour earlier, five o'clock. I said, Yessir, I will, sir, or something like that, and he went off.

Day after that was when they found Tuckie Brenner in Florida.

Florida.

So he ain't around here, that Jimmy Brest, Marvin said. He was driving, looking on at the street. I was looking at the foam piece.

Yeah, I said.

Could be here. Could be in Florida. Could be anywhere.

Yeah, I said.

They hadn't found all Tuckie Brenner, just a piece of'm, and that was three weeks back from when we was driving around now. Took'm three weeks, Florida cops, I mean, to identify out who it was.

We didn't talk about that, though. Just drove. I weren't feeling at all good. I mean I felt real bad, but couldn't say why, and I couldn't talk much, or even look at anybody. And I guess Marvin, he noticed, 'cause after a bit he pulls the van to the side of the street and he stops and looks at me.

Billy?

Yar? I said.

You didn't get along with this Brest boy, did you?

No, I said.

He watched me a minute, Marvin, me just sitting there sort'f blank-faced and staring at the foam piece, and then he talked, low and smooth, almost a whisper to his voice.

Billy, one thing you gotta know is, what you do or say, it don't mean shit 'bout what's real. You understand that?

I didn't say anything and he said, Fact is, you can even kill a man and it ain't real. I mean it ain't nothing you *wanted* to do, ain't nothing you *meant* to do, but just something you *had* to do, 'cause that's the way things were. War taught me that. Life — it all fucked up. Once you know that, things go easier. You can get complicated all you want but that ain't gonna help. You just gotta *know* it. 'Cause what I'm saying is, what you said or done or what he said or done, that don't mean shit now. What you *been* ain't what you *are*. Understand? Most men take their whole life to learn that. But you gotta learn it right now. You hear what I'm saying?

I hear, I said.

So it don't matter what you ever thought about him. You didn't do this, Billy, even if you *wished* it. You understand?

I sat still a minute then, just looking at him, and he never took his eyes off me.

He was right. I *had* wished it.

I fuckin' hated Jimmy Brest.

And he hated me.

Since I was five years old he'd called me the worst names I knew or could remember, for no reason I could ever understand, saying things about my sister and Daddy and even my mother after she died that I could never forget. He hit me and beat on me more times than I could count. But the last thing I wanted, no matter how many times I'd cussed him and said I hated him and wished he was dead, was for him to get anything like what got Tommy Evans. I get mad but I ain't never that mad. So yeah, I was feeling bad 'bout stuff I'd said and thought, and felt guilty for all that.

But maybe those thoughts just hurt too bad, I don't know, 'cause right then they kind'f faded away, and I was thinkin' more about the day before yesterday, before he was took, my mind goin' over all that I'd seen. Last thing I knew he'd done was chase me down that alley into that garage, where I went up the rafters and sat waiting to chuck paint on his fuckin' head should he find me. And there was something else, too, something —

Billy? You all right? Marvin asked me.

I didn't say nothing. He must'f thought I was nuts. But I was staring at that foam piece, thinking, trying to think, to remember about something he had with'm in his hands, that bag of chips he was eating when he chased me, that he never threw down as he ran.

Billy? Marvin's eyes was buggin' now.

Night before last, looking in that car, didn't I see that chip bag? Lying there? Next to Skugger's goofball hat?

Didn't I?

I knew then I had to see that car again, see if it was still there.

Marvin, now he shoves my shoulder. You okay, Billy?

I'm fine, Marvin, I say.

Damn, boy, he says. You was in a *trance* or something!

I guess I sort'f grinned at'm. Then I said, Marvin?

Yeah?

I wanna find'm.

Marvin nods his head and from off the dashboard he takes one of them cigarettes he smokes 'bout once every two weeks when he's thinking hard. Real slow he lights it, and then he looks at me and says, That would mean a lot to you, that right, Billy?

To *me?* How you mean?

His face sort'f pinches. He says, People might think a lot different 'bout you if you done a thing like that. Might forgive you a lot. Ain't that what you was thinking about just now?

Yeah, Marvin, I say. Sure. That's just it.

And it was, a little. But even more I was thinking about that chip bag, wonderin' if I could get hold of it.

He smiles, sad smile sort'f. Puffs out some smoke and says, That'll be hard, Billy. Findin' him. That gonna take *double* luck. And that shit just don't happen.

Why so? I said.

'Cause the money, he said.

'Cause I ain't told you. At the bottom of that flyer, under Jimmy Brest's face and the day he was took and what he was wearing and how old he was, there was wrote something else.

ONE HUNDRED THOUSAND DOLLARS REWARD.

Findin' him, findin' him alive, Marvin said, that's *luck*. But gettin' the money, too, that's *double* luck. That's like a lotto ticket that wins twice, and that shit don't happen. Fact is, they shouldn't've put up the money, 'cause ain't nobody gonna ever get it, he said.

Yeah, you prob'ly right, I said.

'Cept maybe the grave digger, he said, and we went driving on.

PART TWO

CHAPTER FOURTEEN

Here's how I had it.

Maybe the chip bag was in that car. Say it was.

And maybe it was the same I'd seen Brest had when he chased me.

So what?

Could'f come from anywheres. 'Cause it just a chip bag, don't mean nothing.

'Cept to me it did, and here's what. Meant maybe that I saw Skugger in that car, and he was high, smoking dope all day with the man driving. And he tells about Brest wanting to find me and then flips me the bird, Skugger does. I cuss him good for that, so he calls Brest on his cell phone maybe, and Brest finds me quick and chases my ass. And he got them chips with'm, munching on the goddamn things as he's running along after me. I get away, but Brest, he calls Skugger back, and Skugger comes to give'm a ride. Then they both go off to party somewheres with the man, and Brest leaves them chips he was eating in the car, and Skugger leaves his hat.

Damn. Getting all that straight in my mind almost gave me a headache. But I was thinking, maybe this was the *last* time anybody seen'm, seen Jimmy Brest, I mean. Course I couldn't prove nothing, and what was there to prove? Can you 'magine me walking in the police station holding some chip bag and saying it belonged to Jimmy Brest? But along with the boxes and the mittens and the car and the man, it all might add up if I was sure it was the same bag I'd seen Brest holding when he chased me.

So just to be sure, I had to see that car again.

When Marvin dropped me off it was still afternoon and instead of going home I went to the dark house. I walked past looking at it for just a second, 'cause I didn't know if anybody was inside and I be damned to let'm catch me spyin'. But there weren't no sign of anybody, and I was thinking of sneaking around back to see if the car was there, but tell the truth I was a little worried to do it by daylight.

Then I hear a noise comin' up the street, noise goes, *swap!* Then a minute passes and you hear another *swap!* I turn around fast and what I see is my boy Sam Tate coming up the middle of the street, chucking his papers at houses both sides.

When he comes by I say, Hey, Sam, c'mere a minute, I gotta ask you something.

Hi, Billy, he says, and he comes on over.

Now Sam Tate, he's my friend. Got long hair, blond like me just longer, and he's about my size, which ain't tall, but he got a face which I swear looks like a church angel, it's so straight and regular and not like mine which is all stubby and beat. He sort'f likes me. He ain't like the average boy around here, I mean all snooty. First, his daddy's crazy. Yells at him all the time, a sort of yelling that drove Sam's mother away and his brother and sister, too, until now it's just Sam in the house with his daddy climbing the walls from all those bad memories he got, 'cause that's what I s'pose Sam's daddy has, bad memories, I mean.

I heard him yelling. Won't deny it. Used to hide in the bushes out front of the house just to hear. And he could *yell*, believe me. Whole neighborhood knows. It's so fuckin' loud is why. Sort of like he got a terror in him. But I won't say what it's all about, the yelling, I mean. That's nosy. You go ask Sam Tate if you really wanna know.

Funny thing is I never heard *Sam* yell. In the house I heard him screaming and crying, but never outside. Outside he's calm as could be, and quiet and real inside himself, and don't hardly talk at all. Some boys think that's funny and it do make me smile, until I think how Sam feels inside.

You see, me, I got scars on my face. But this Sam Tate, this friend of mine? All his scars are on his heart.

Still, he really easy to fool, and I played tricks on'm plenty of times, can't help it. You just listen to this.

Sam, I said, duck on down! Come inside here.

I was acting really sneaky and I'd figured he'd go for that, so what I did was duck down'n he did too and followed me inside a hedge about four/five foot, where we sat in a clear space where nobody could see us, even walking right by.

What is it? Sam said, sitting there picking prickles off his shirt.

I waited a second before I talked, looking up through the bush brambles at the house now again like I was waiting for something to happen, looking at a front window that didn't have no cover inside and let on to an empty room. Then I looked at Sam.

You know that boy Skugger, right?

Yeah, Sam said.

Know him good?

We don't hang out like we used to. He does different stuff now, Sam said.

I knew that meant they weren't good friends 'cause he weren't ole Skugger's drug buddy.

But you still see'm, right?

Yeah, now and then. What's up?

I want you to do something for me. Skugger's been driving around in this blue car, you seen it?

Oh yeah. Plenty of times, he said.

Do me a favor, next time you see Skugger, ask him who owns that car, will ya?

I know who it is already, Billy, Sam said. It's the guy who sells him drugs.

So I was right about that, I'm thinking.

I say, You know his name?

I never met him, Sam said.

Try, I say. Try'n meet'm. He won't meet me 'cause Skugger don't like me. But if you do it I'll have something for you. Something good.

What?

Don't know yet, but *something,* I say.

Sam looks sad a minute. You aren't doing drugs, are you, Billy? Because if that's what it is, I don't want any.

No way! I says. Never done'm! Ain't gonna sell'm, neither, that ain't why I'm asking. I just want to know what his name is, if you can manage it.

All right, Sam said. When I see Skugger I'll ask him.

Knowing Sam like I do and how he wants boys to like'm, I hold up a minute. I know he might just walk right on up to Skugger and say, Hey, Skugger, who's that man you hanging with, Billy Zeets wants to know. So I take Sam's arm and look at'm tight. Just do it on the sly, I said. Don't go saying it's me that's askin', you hear? And if you can, try'n find out where he lives, will ya? It ain't for nothing bad, I promise you. Will you help me?

Sam said yeah, he'd try. Then he got up out the bushes. I've got to finish my route, he told me. Curfew's coming.

Thanks, buddy, I said, and I squeezed his arm again and he smiled.

He went up the street and I saw him tossing papers all going *swap, swap,* and then he walked down to the bottom of the hill and it was like them trees rose over his head'n swallowed him.

I turned back around, real sudden. Watchin' Sam walk off, something had caught me out the corner of my eye. So one last time I looked up at the house.

A man stood at that window, the man from the car. I seen him just a second, before he pulled down that tarp and disappeared.

I stood a minute, staring, feeling cold all over. Then I started on home, walking down the middle of the street, faster than usual. Every few feet I looked behind myself, though that didn't slow my walking.

And once or twice . . .

I started runnin'.

I was prob'ly just seeing things, 'cause'f shadows on the street.

But the feeling I had was that this man I wanted to find was now trying to find *me*.

CHAPTER FIFTEEN

I got home all sweaty, and all I done was go upstairs and rest until dark. I ain't one for getting scared, I guess you know that. But this man I seen was bugging me out. Fact is, Sam and me in the bushes couldn't be seen from the street, but anybody in the house could'f looked right down and seen us fine, and maybe even heard a word or two. So I was worried, and knew damn well somebody followed me partways home, 'cause I got a sense for that.

Something weird was going on. I mean, them mittens struck me as weird and that blue car struck me as weird and so did the chip bag. I felt so damn confused. It was like when you in class and just staring at your desk and not listening and then all a sudden the nun prods you and asks you for the answer, asks just because you ain't been listening, and you get all startled and try to remember, and maybe if you had a spare hour you *would* remember, remember what you sort'f heard but didn't pay attention to, 'cause you heard it just the same. But you never do get that hour and so you hear everybody say you ain't nothing but a dummy and laughs all round the class.

Them things like the mittens and the boxes and the chip bag, they was like them answers you sort'f heard but can't remember, and you gotta give'm time to come up.

So what I done was lay still, waiting for them answers.

But I didn't get no time 'cause right then I heard a sound from out the hall, a sort of mewling like a cat'll make. And I sat up 'cause I knew it was Leezie crying outside my door.

I looked over. Made me miserable to hear her. Weren't the first time, neither. Going past'r door at night I'd heard her cry plenty'f times, 'specially nights since that mortgage letter come. Most days she was angry and bossy, and really sort'f pickin' on me 'cause she was so damn antsy. She spent most'f her nights out, but the nights she stayed home she was always shut up in her room all alone. And she never did try'n get a job or nothing. Had me thinkin' she was too sad to get busy, 'cause all our troubles just broke her down.

Leezie? I say. You out there?

My room was dark now, and Leezie come in. First she opened the door and just said, Billy? and I said, Yar? because I could hear already she was crying again. She was standing there at the door with just the hall light behind her. I could only see her outline, rest of her was dark, and I could even see her hair, which was hanging loose and stringy, which was odd because Leezie, she's a real pretty girl and likes to take care of herself, but there you go.

I reached out and she said, Leave the light off, and I said, Sure. Then she comes over to me and sits and I edge over. I could see she was holding something in her hand. Looked like an ink pen. But it was too dark to tell, 'cause she'd shut the door behind herself coming in.

Why you crying, Leezie? I said.

She didn't say nothing and the window was open, little glow of the community center lights out there through the trees, and a cool breeze coming, 'cause the hot day had settled down.

Do you love me, Billy? she said.

Hell yeah, I said.

Don't curse, she said.

Scuze my language, I said. But yeah, I love you lots.

Well I love you too, Billy, she said. Or she tried to say it, getting past the choke in'r voice. I know I ain't helped you none with making any money, she says. I'm just so scared, Billy. And I been really mean to you this summer. I'm sorry.

Ain't even noticed, I say.

Then she says, Billy?

Uh-huh?

Look at this, she said. She meant the thing she was holdin' in'r hand, ink-pen thing. She held it up.

I can't see it, I said, and I reached aside. Lemme turn —

Leave it off! she said.

Okay, I said.

Just look at it, she said.

I did. I leaned over, right over her lap. She didn't smell like nothing. I mean she smelled like herself. I mean she didn't have no perfume on, and was just good ole Leezie again. Thought I'd mention that.

I looked. Looked hard. Couldn't see a goddamn thing.

Keep looking, she said.

I did. And there it was. In that ink-pen-shaped thing she held, cigar-shaped thing, there it was.

Little plus sign.

Little glow-in-the-dark plus sign, that you saw better when you weren't looking straight at it but a little off to the side.

It's a plus sign, I said. Ain't it?

She tried to say something but all she did was cry and

breathe fast and grab at me. Then she tried again and still couldn't.

You right now are prob'ly looking at me thinkin' I'm dumb because of course everybody knows what the plus sign means. But at that moment I didn't *want* to know and didn't care if I *did* know. I figured what with everything else going on I just weren't *interested* in knowing.

Sure, I see it, I said. What it mean?

It means I'm having a baby, she said. She was calm all a sudden.

Where'd you get this doohickey? How's it work?

Bought it at Shatze's, she said. I had to pee on it.

Yeah? I said. What if I pee on it? That gonna make the minus sign show up?

Billy! she said.

Okay, I said, thinking it's prob'ly best not to joke with'r.

What you gonna do about it? I said.

She trembled. I don't *know!* I'm going to have to leave school! Oh Lord, what would Mommy say? Everyone will know!

You can't worry about that, Leezie, I said. And Mommy, well, you never was no trouble for'r like I was. She'd prob'ly just say she loves you. I mean, once she was done bein' mad atchu.

110

She was sniffin' then, but at that last I said she laughed a little.

Then I waited a minute and said, You gonna go 'head with it?

She knew what I meant. Because her face flashed at me and even through the dark I could see the look on it, and she said, *Yes yes yes!* like she'd scratch me if I asked again.

Up till now she'd seemed lost, Leezie had. But right then I felt I had her back again and she'd be okay. 'Cause that's her way, like I told you, and just how she gets when there's something she wants.

Then you go right ahead, I said.

She got up. But before she left I said, You told Ricky yet?

Yes, she said.

What's he say?

Says he loves me, she said.

Me, I'm thinking he damn well better, 'cause if that boy plays round with my sister I'll set fire to his ass 'fore he can take a piss to put it out.

There's one thing else, she said. I can't stay here. Not with the baby coming. I can't do that to you and Daddy.

Why not? Leezie, you got to stay.

She shook her head. You got enough trouble on your hands.

What you gonna do? I said.

Try living with Ricky, she said, her voice quiet. He got a house all his own, him and his brothers.

He gonna let you?

She looked at me. Do he got a choice? she said, and I damn near laughed at how hard she sounded.

He knows I gotta move in, she said, a little softer. We already talked about it.

He's a wild boy, Leezie. I wouldn't do it.

He's different with me, Billy. He promised me he'll change his ways.

I shook my head at that. In my mind, ain't nothing gonna make that boy simmer down.

It would have happened anyway, she said, even if we weren't losing the house. I love him, Billy. You get older you'll understand.

I smiled a little. I didn't have to get no older to know that maybe some ways she was just thinkin' the best thing now was to get with someone else or start livin' somewhere else. I'd known something had been on her mind a while, maybe this was it.

He gonna treat you nice?

I can handle him. He'll do anything I say.

She was talking big but I knew him better in a lot

of ways. I was worried, I'll tell you. I hoped she wouldn't really do it.

She waits a sec, then she says real quiet, Billy, maybe you, well, they got extra rooms, and if—

I smiled bigger. So it was that, too. Finding me a place, like it's her way of looking after me. Well, it was nice'f her to think of getting me somewhere to live, though I couldn't see myself livin' with Bad-Ass—no fuckin' way. But I didn't say nothing.

Well, I ain't gave up on this house yet, Leezie, I said. And Daddy, he got this idea for us having a fruit stand? I figure that's something I want too, so I best stick around.

She looks at me and touches my hand. I can't help with that, Billy, she says. And she's sad sayin' it.

She stepped away. I wait till she's at the door and then I say, I bet you gonna have a sweet little girl.

Hall light on her face, she said, I don't know if it's a girl or a boy, Billy. I ain't seen the doctor yet.

No, I said. It's a girl. I *know* it.

How?

I sort'f sat up on my shoulders, elbows, I mean.

'Cause this world don't need another Bad-Ass Ricky, I said.

Billy! she said. And then she went out my room.

CHAPTER SIXTEEN

Not too much news came my way for the next month or so. I saw Sam a couple times when he was out on his paper route. He hadn't managed to see Skugger yet. I told him to hurry his ass up, but he said he'd asked around a bit and learned Skugger had gone away on vacation with his parents, somewhere down Mexico, Sam said, and wouldn't be back till the end of the month. Twice I seen that car drive by with the man in it, but I always ducked away fast 'cause it seemed too damn risky to try'n follow him. Going around I kept both eyes open, 'cause since that day at the dark house it's like I was feeling watched everywhere I went. I never looked to see if the chip bag was still in the car, just didn't seem safe. And the weeks kept passin', with our day to get out the house coming up fast, and me with nothing like the sort'f money we needed to stay there.

I kept up working all the same, mowing lawns and doing house jobs and going round with Marvin and Richie all through June and July. Just so you know, working all them days I made twenty-three hundred dollars. Ain't forty-eight thousand, that's for damn sure. I was real unhappy about coming up short. Most days after I'd finished work I'd sit on a curb thinking it over, what to do with all that money, I mean. I even prayed, even though it might not do no good, me bein' me and all.

One thing I remembered was how I used to help out selling stuff at this weekend market them nuns do downtown at school, and I remembered all that cash stuffed in my pockets by noontime. So I was thinking maybe to ask Richie to help me think of something to buy and sell, and sign the permit to do it, 'cause I ain't old enough, and you gotta have one, permit, I mean, taped to your table elsewise them police gonna shut you down. And I kept thinking too 'bout what my daddy said about the fruit stand and I tell you, more'n more I come to think it was a damn good idea. I ain't never been much at school, why not start working right now?

I went'n talked to Daddy about it. He was in the hallway downstairs, and he smiled and said he was glad I was askin', and seemed to come alive a little. He talked some about how my mother always said she wanted us to work together someday, but then he shook his head and said what I got ain't enough. Need at least ten thousand stake to start up, he said, that's what the man at the fish store told'm, so I had to go back a step, and keep thinking 'bout what to buy and sell with Richie Harrigan.

But God damn. Twenty-three hundred dollars. Can you beat that? Any other summer I'd'f been clicking my heels, 'cause keeping it all for myself I could'f bought a goddamn *car* if I wanted. Used one, I mean.

I knew by now I couldn't make the mortgage. But I still kept up mowing lawns and asking around at houses. Figured at least I could pay a couple months' apartment rent when the house was gone. And anyway I liked working and feeling that money in my pocket.

Roundabout the end of July I was mowing a lawn, Old Man Highdale's over on Oakley Drive, and he was paying forty dollars for front and back 'cause his yard's so goddamn big. It's a push mower and I was pushing, sweat coming all down my face and feeling the heat, when I hear a voice say, Hey, Billy! I look up and see Sam Tate coming at me from crost the street, a big smile on his face like he finally got something to tell me. So I stop a sec and say, Hiya, Sam, and when he gets to me he says real loud, *I saw Skugger and the man's name is* —

I grab his arm and say, Hold up! Don't go talking out here! Walk a ways with me.

Sam, he looks confused, but still holding his arm I take'm round back where Highdale got one of them metal sheds, sort you buy down HomeWorld and build yourself for storing your rakes and clippers in.

I shut the door and it's dark in there 'cept for what's creeping in the seams where it's bolted, and it's sort'f damp and way too warm and smells like them bags of potters' soil Highdale uses in 's garden. Sam, he still looks a little uncertain of what I'm up to, so I let go his arm and say real soft, I just don't want nobody to hear, might think I'm nosy. So tell me what you got.

Sam says, His name is Hodsworth. Peter Hodsworth.

Where's he from? I ask.

I don't know. Skugger didn't say.

Where's he live?

He didn't say that either. But when we all got together—

You got *together?!*

Yeah, Sam said. He smiled. Wasn't I supposed to?

Well, yeah, but . . . How's Skugger know'm?

He didn't say that, either.

What the hell *did* he say?

Well, we went to the park.

What park?

Robert E. Lee, Sam said.

Now, I know you know Robert E. Lee Park. That's the big park with the lake, and railroad tracks and rock cliffs, and so many trees and winding paths you can hide yourself so nobody'll ever find you. Lots'f boys go there to party, ain't no secret.

Okay, Robert E. Lee. And what he say?

They just joked a lot and didn't say much of anything, Sam said, his face now getting sort'f pinched-looking realizing how little he'd learned.

I said, Did they say anything about Jimmy Brest?

No, Sam said. But I did. I talked about how scary it was, all these kids getting taken, and what sort of things probably happen to the kids, and how great it would be to bring one of them back alive. Skugger thought so too.

I looked at him steady and there didn't seem to be nothing else on his mind about it, I mean he didn't suspect Hodsworth of anything, and hadn't felt no danger.

I asked, This man Hodsworth say anything about Brest?

No, Sam said. He just sat there smoking a jay. They were so high everything seemed funny. And when Hodsworth went off to go to the bathroom Skugger said he gets pot and pills from people downtown. Said he thinks he maybe works at a hospital, or knows people who do, because the pills are always in those orange bottles.

Vials, I say.

Yeah, vials, Sam says.

Hmm, Peter Hodsworth, I said, like saying the name out loud might mean something to me. But it didn't.

It all seemed so empty to me I felt angry and all I wanted was to get back to mowin' Highdale's yard. So we went out over the lawn back to the mower. Sam said bye and was going to the street, but when he was at the sidewalk he turned to me.

There's one thing, he said. His car.

What about it? I said.

You know, I never saw it parked on the street. But I know where he parks it.

Where at?

You know that hill over Church Lane? Where the woods begin?

I know it, I said.

That's where, Sam said. Maybe he lives around there.

And he walked on.

After I got done at Highdale's I got the forty and went home. Was getting close to curfew so I walked fast, all the while tryin' to grab hold the thoughts runnin' through my head. What Sam had said didn't mean jack shit to me, or didn't seem to. I kept thinking there's something I oughta remember but I can't, something I'd seen or heard. But the more I tried the further it went, so after a while I gave up, hoping it was just gonna pop on out without me even trying. Course I felt bad Sam got in the man's car, Hodsworth's car. That seemed risky and it worried me—and when you get right down to it, I was the only one to blame for his having gone and done it in the first place.

Daddy was back in the kitchen working at a crossword with dim lamplight on'm, didn't seem to give a damn we was losing the house in four weeks. I got a little to eat, larder stuff, peanut butter and crackers, and some of that log cheese. Leezie weren't home, she was out with Bad-Ass, that's what Daddy said, and I felt pretty bad about that. Then I went up to my room.

I sat there thinking, but there was nothing to think.

What Sam said didn't sound just right to me. I had the notion that if it'd been me sittin' there with'm, I'd'f seen something he hadn't noticed, but I couldn't say what it was.

So what the hell was I doing? What was I looking for?

Who was this Hodsworth? Why's he living in that dark house, or at least going in it, moving the boxes and such? He drives boys around, smoking dope with'm so they forget themselves and leave things in his car, and I knew one of them boys was Jimmy Brest.

I had an idea of what I was thinking. Just was afraid of saying it to myself. I got the idea when I first saw the boxes and the boys' clothes on the floor. Got it harder when I seen the same boxes in Miss Gurpy's house and wondered why they was there. Got it hardest of all seeing that man sneaking around his yard with the lights off so nobody sees him, 'cept for me 'cause I'm the one up in the tree fort watchin'm. Did he know Miss Gurpy? And what if he did? I couldn't figure nothing he was doing, and it bothered me good, even taking my mind off losing the house and Leezie getting herself into a mess with Bad-Ass. And since I'd seen Sam and learned the man's name, it was coming even stronger.

But I still couldn't say it. It'd be like just saying anything off the top of your head when the nun prods you, and you know beforehand it gonna be wrong.

'Cause I always had the wrong answers. Just said anything to get it all the hell over with.

But this time I had to be *right*.

So I went through it, again and again, trying to answer it.

'Cause there was another man too. A man killing boys like Tommy Evans, and Tuckie Brenner who was cut up in Florida.

So I couldn't help thinking.

Was they the *same* man?

I had to find out.

Didn't do me much good thinking that way, 'cause there was nothing I could do about it.

'Cept maybe one thing.

Scary thing, and I tried not to think about it.

But then I thought, *Why the hell not?*

I got my ass out'f bed and went to the window. Was dark out there. Curfew was up and I had to be careful, so I went out the window and over the roof, then down the wood stairs back of my house, same as how I used to sneak out nights. Went through the yard and when I got to the alley, I ran.

I got to Church Lane in maybe ten minutes, runnin' through backyards all the way. It was real dark up there, and I climbed the hill. When I get up top I climb a tree. Looking over, I see I'm just level with Miss Gurpy's attic, where I cleaned the gutters, me being high on the hill now and in the tree. Below me is where the woods start and the wood trail ends, just where Sam Tate tells me this man Hodsworth parks his car.

I needed answers and this was all I could think to do to get'm. I weren't sure what I was doing, but just tryin' to add up something stuck in the back of my mind.

It must'f added up good, though, 'cause after 'bout five minutes I hear a car coming, tires crackling over the sticks and bramble on the trail, and it stops just there below me, no headlights on so's nothing shining on the trees.

I held my goddamn breath and watched. The door opens and there he comes, the man, Peter Hodsworth. He's alone, ain't got Skugger with'm. What he does is lock his car and go to the edge of the hill, where old rotty stairs come up from Miss Gurpy's. He goes down those stairs and I can hardly see'm and then I can't see'm at all, darkness like a pool 'cause she ain't got no outside house lights. But I hear'm get to her backyard porch and in he goes, and I know now he got his own key.

I get down that tree and in a flash I'm at that car 'cause I want a look inside, to see if maybe that chip bag is still there. But the doors'r locked and I can't see nothing. Then a light catches my eyes. I look over. Attic light at Miss Gurpy's shines on, I can see the square of the window through the black of the bramble. And I stand there, my mouth hanging open.

He's hiding *things in there,* I'm thinking. *Taking things from the other house and hiding them here.*

What's *he hiding?*

For a minute more I watch him, 'cause inside there I see his shape through the window. Then I turn to run like hell.

But I don't run. This man, he might be watchin' me, I think. Following me in the neighborhood, watchin' me mow lawns. He followed me that first day I talked to Sam in the bushes, and I seen'm drive by a couple times since and maybe it's on purpose.

So he got to know *I'm* watchin' *him*.

I kneel down and do to that car something I ain't done for two years to *no* car, ever since my mother died. I pull off both sideviews and bend up the wipers. Fucked it up good, scuze my language. That's something I used to think was fun, don't ask why, I couldn't tell you.

But I ain't doing it for fun now.

I'm doing it to *scare.*

Then I run like hell, and I get home soon and back in the window to my room, lying in bed, breathing hard, and thinking, *I got to get in that damn Miss Gurpy's house.*

CHAPTER SEVENTEEN

I wanted to ask Richie what to buy with the twenty-three hundred I'd made, tell'm 'bout the fruit stand and hear what he thinks, so I went out early looking for'm. Found him up on the avenue loading an old washing machine in the bed of his pickup. He do that sometimes 'cause just for bringing in a busted one, used one, a store'll give him cash money. Some people collect them old machines, but most folks, 'specially those as had'm a while too long, just see'm as junk.

Hey, Monkey Boy, he said through his teeth without no other hello, steady that ramp, will ya?

I done it, come up behind his pickup and leaned hard on the ramp, which was a old door, laid straight down from the bed. I could tell he was in a bad mood 'cause he smacked that washing machine around harder than he had to, and didn't say a word while we worked. With me holding the ramp it didn't take long for him to get it up, and after we'd tied it down we both got in and was soon going downtown t'where them used-appliance shops is.

He sat driving, window open, wind blowin' through that short-cut hair of his, lit cigarette stuck in his mouth, burning, that he never took out and made his eyes squint and water a little. His T-shirt was white and had big stains, oil stains, and no sleeves 'cause he'd ripped'm off, strings hanging loose. He took hard turns and I had to hold on, and once I even heard the washing machine slide a little over loose lumber he got in the bed.

Whoa, hold on! I yelled.

He laughed a little, not looking at me.

How you doin', Monkey Boy? he says, voice all hard.

Good, I says. How 'bout you?

Me? Shit. Who wants to know?

Now he looked at me, quick, that sunburned face of his all scowly, eyes pinched.

He says, I spent all last night in *jail,* Monkey Boy. Whole night. Took my daddy and three lawyers to get me out. That surprised those fuckin' cops, I'll tell you that.

Jesus, I said. What all happened?

He laughed again, short and nasty.

They pulled me in. *Suspicion.*

Suspicion for what? I say.

What the hell you think? For killing those boys.

Who the hell thought that?

That fucker Officer Dryker, he said.

I know'm, I said.

He came and got me, Richie gasped. Right out back my *father's* house. My father saw him cuff me and take me 'way. I almost smacked the fucker, but his damn fool partner was there with his goddamn hand on his gun.

That's all Richie said about getting busted, because now he turns his face to me and there was a look in his eyes I can't hardly say. It was mad but also sort of teary, and his voice was breaking when he yelled. And all this while he's just driving like a crazy man.

Who the hell would think *I* took those boys! he yelled, his voice the same as crying, and dropping a hand from the wheel to smack hisself on the chest. If there's *anything* like a watchdog in this neighborhood it's *me,* not that damn asshole Dryker! All night they talked at me, wanting to know where I was and what I was doing, sometimes a whole year back! I—I—

Why'd they'd come? I said.

You know *why!* he said. 'Cause of that day I beat his ass! Jimmy pussy-ass Brest! Some damn lady saw me, out her damn kitchen window. She didn't see you 'cause you was lying on the ground with your nose busted! I didn't even say you were there!

Should'f told, I said. I'd of come down.

He hit the wheel now, thumped it, jumped a stoplight and swerved fast round this car he almost hit, then poked his head out the window and yelled, *DRIVE RIGHT, YOU FUCKER!* Then looking ahead he's breathin' fast and sayin', Man, I oughta turn back around and kick that fucker's ass!

But he didn't stop, thank the Lord.

It's all right, Richie, I say. Nobody's gonna think you did anything.

He looked at me. *Yeah?* Bullshit! They're *all* gonna think it! Who *am* I? Used to drink, quit college, I haul garbage! All I *am* is this neighborhood, I got nothing else!

Nobody will think it, Richie, I said. Dryker's a fuckin' nut.

Richie didn't talk now, just shook, something I seen him do before. Strong a man as he is, I think that drinking he used to do hurt his head, and there're some things he just can't figure out, 'specially when's he's bothered.

Dryker talked to me, too, I said, and I was telling true,

because about a week before I'd stopped him on the street and asked him some questions.

I told him I wanted to catch who's taking the boys, I said. Know what he told me? Said he didn't want to hear none of my accusations, like I even had any or if I did I'd just tell'm to lie about people. Laughed right in my face. Said what I had to have was *proof*. I said, What proof? Know what he said? He said, The man himself, that's all I'll take from you.

He's an asshole, Monkey Boy, Richie said. But you're right. Only way to do it is catch him. Somebody's *got* to catch him. Only way to clear my name!

We dropped the washer at All Brand Appliances down at Twenty-Eight and Calvert, and Richie got forty dollars for it, which had me wishin' I had three/four hundred old washing machines. Then we headed on back, him still in the same sort of pissed-off cocky mood he'd been in before, his face with that tight-grin look and wide-awake eyes like he *expected* shit to happen, and was maybe like one clock-tick away from *making* shit happen.

I didn't see that going away, his mood, I mean, but I could see he was feelin' a little more used to having been chucked in jail, and the main thing he did, now that he was back in the neighborhood, was look long at any neighbors when he passed'm on their lawns, and slow down going by them, giving them a kind of hard-starey eyeball, as if the whole neighborhood and not just one dumbass cop had accused him of bein' a child killer.

That was his way and I didn't say nothing, till I said, Richie, you gonna help me with something?

Yeah? he said.

I got twenty-three hundred dollars. 'S what I made this summer. I gotta make it make more. Buy something and sell it.

What you want to buy?

Don't know yet, I said.

Having something other to think about sort of cooled him, I could tell. He thought a minute driving along, and then looked over at me.

Hmm. Buy and sell. Where at?

Downtown market. We'll make a bundle.

Again he thought a minute, sometimes his face looking serious, other times grinning and laughing a little like he thinks what I'm saying is a joke.

Finally he says to me, Nah, I can't do it right now. I got a big job. Hauling. And that's something we gotta talk about.

What's there to talk about? I say. 'Cause me, I'm

thinking I really don't want to spend a day with Richie hauling for chump change when I could start on making some big money.

I really need the money *now,* I say. For saving my daddy's house! Won't you help me? I can't sign the permit myself!

Richie, he grins a little hearing 'bout the house, 'cause he already told me he don't think I can make all that money. Then he says, Well, this gonna take just a day or two. And you won't be hauling. I need you for something different. You don't do it I gotta ask Skugger, and that boy don't know how to work. Anyway it ain't a problem for you. You already know the lady.

Who's that?

Now he grins real wide. Miss Gurpy.

I couldn't say nothing, just stare. He looked at how surprised I was and laughed right at me.

Now don't go thinking I swiped the job from you! he says. You're the one who told me 'bout clearin' her gutters! So I went by and asked about her whole house. It's filled up with forty years' worth of junk! She gotta clear it 'cause she'll get an injunction and get put in a nursing home, 's all she can talk about! That's something *you* put in'r head! She doesn't want that sort of trouble, Monkey Boy. Anyway I'm no stranger to her. I worked a little for'r a couple years ago.

I took a second to catch my breath. I was gonna get a chance at looking at them boxes! I felt like yelling right then and there.

You say you got room for me on it? I asked.

Sure, Monkey Boy, but why you changin' your mind? I thought you were so hot to double that twenty-three hundred?

For a second I couldn't explain myself. Felt like a damn fool for having ever said no. I didn't wanna answer too quick or say too much, 'cause it wouldn't do having him thinkin' I'm antsy to get in there, and have'm start asking questions.

So I waited a minute and sort'f moved my shoulders like maybe I didn't care about nothing. Then I said, sort'f sputtered, Well, you'll do the other thing after, the market, I mean?

Sure, if you're still up to it. You coming on with me? I'm starting tomorrow, and you know what she says she's got?

What's that? I ask.

Rats, he said, grinning crazy.

No *way,* I say.

Oh c'mon, Monkey Boy! He was laughing now. What, you wanna say no again? His voice is sort of happy now, like he thought rats was something I wanted to hear about. And for a sec he took his hands off the wheel and held'm up 'bout two foot apart.

He says, *Big* ones. Big fucking nasty rats, and she's right, too, 'cause she had me in yesterday and I seen the rat shit all over, them little black peas. Whole attic, Monkey Boy! Wanna help me do it? I'm gonna need a hand for rats.

I don't know, I say. How much you payin'?

Give you a hundred. Ain't a rip-off. I got truck costs and expenses.

How we gonna do it? I say.

Shit, he said, smiling, looking down. Same as before.

With a *gun?* That shit's crazy, I said. I'm still picking pellets out my ass from the last time!

He looked up bright, eyes like half-crazy, that frazzle he gets sometimes. No, Monkey Boy! I got a new one! I hold the gun, you flick the lights! What else you want to do? Use traps? That'll never work, damn rats are too smart. And we can't use poison. Old Gurpy'll probably eat it herself. C'mon, he said, that grin still on his face lighting up his eyes. Another hundred'll help that buy-and-sell thing you want to do.

I shook my head a little. Being in an attic with Richie

Harrigan and a gun weren't something to take lightly. But I couldn't skip a chance of seeing all what's up there.

I nodded. All right, I said. But I *am* gonna stand behind you.

Sure you are! he said. And he smacked my shoulder with his hand like to seal the deal, too hard I thought, and we went driving on.

CHAPTER EIGHTEEN

Coming home I let the screen door bang shut, and I saw my daddy. He was coming up from the kitchen, wearing one of them check shirts he wears, baggy one, and his cheeks was just gray grizzle 'cause he ain't shaved, and his eyeglasses shine like chrome rings on his face. He looked a little jolted to see me, like I busted in on his thoughts.

Oh, hi, son, he says. Help me here, will you?

I don't move. I'm looking at him, then down at something I don't believe I see.

Boxes.

At his feet are about twenty of'm, all cardboard and cut down flat, so now what he's doing is taking this roll of packing tape and making them all back again, folding the flaps and taping them down.

Daddy, what're you doing?

He's still looking at me, face just as gray as his hair.

I'm gonna pack, son. Start it, anyway. We'll need more boxes when move time comes.

Move time? I say.

He don't say nothing for a minute. Stares at me.

That ain't necessary, I say. Daddy, we still got more'n three weeks! It's wrong to do this! You can't just give up! We gotta *do* something —

Billy, he says, you can't make the money in three weeks. The house belongs to the bank now. It ain't mine no more.

You worked twenty years for it, I say.

Billy —

Twenty years, I say.

Now he looks down at the boxes at his feet, and the others he already taped and folded, stacked against the wall there.

Leezie left, he said quietly. She told me 'bout the baby. She gone to live with Ricky.

This time I didn't say nothing. Even though I'd known it was coming, I couldn't believe she'd really gone and done it. First my mother dies — now Leezie goes. It was like my whole family was over and done with.

I just stood there looking at the floor, the floor of worn

planks Daddy never shellacked or repainted 'cause he was always working on other people's houses. I sort of let out a breath, and then I went out the hall to the living room where I dropped on the sofa, that sofa I'd found in an alley thrown out a few years ago and that Richie Harrigan and me'd brung in the house, 'cause we never had th'money to buy a new one.

I looked at Daddy.

Leezie's livin' with Bad-Ass? I said, like I ain't heard.

Yes, he said.

You know he got brothers? I asked.

She didn't say, he said.

I knew a boy who drowned once. He was my age, and he jumped in the water down Robert E. Lee Park, jumped off that railroad bridge. Banged his head going in. Didn't knock him out, but it did make him breathe when he was underwater, and his lungs filled. We dragged him out, and thank the Lord there was a doctor having a picnic 'bout twenty yards away, and he run up. First he looked real doubtful, 'cause he saw the blood on the boy's face and figured he was dead, but he gave him mouth-to-mouth anyway, and it saved him. Boy was Sam Tate. And you know what he said? He said it weren't bad, drowning. He'd gone faint right off the bat, and weren't bothered. What hurt like hell was the water coming out, he said.

And me, I'm bringing this up 'cause for a second there, after hearing Leezie had really gone and done it, I was gonna say some such thing like I felt I was drowning, but that ain't so. Because with drowning, you dead in a minute and don't give a shit no more. But with the shit I was hearing, death would never come and it was all just gonna go on forever.

She can't live there! I yelled. His brothers are worse than him! One's a goddamn Marine Corps ranger! She talks big like she can handle it, but what if she can't! What if they beat her and call her names and make her do all the work, and all have their nasty way with'r when Ricky gets sick of'r! How the hell you let'r go!?

Everything I yelled seemed to hit him hard, so I shut up.

She can take care of herself, he says, his voice so weak I hardly hear'm. Then he looks straight at me, his face full of pain, and says, She's strong, Billy. Strong like your mother was.

Right then I didn't care how strong she was. My head felt on fire. Yeah! How do you know?! All you done for the last year is sit around doin' nothing! You hardly even talked with'r!

I couldn't stop her, son. And she's right. We *all* have to go.

Where we gonna live?! I say.

I don't know, he says.

Then he looked up. I—I know about a place downtown. Sober men's housing.

Daddy, that's ridiculous! Living with them drunks, you'll start up again, I *know* it.

He acted like he didn't hear what I said, and just said, I heard about it at my AA. It's only a hundred a week.

Yeah?! My brain felt hot, my face, too. What about the goddamn house and the fruit stand! Ain't you even gonna *try!* What *about* it!

I don't know, son. I—I—

He looked like he was falling apart, gray and small and weak and old, and his clothes all wrinkled, wrinkled as his skin, and it looking gray and dead too.

AND WHAT ABOUT *ME!* I yelled.

And that's when he started crying, just an old gray man shaking and crying, not making a sound but his body rumplin' like he wanted to die.

I don't *know,* son! I don't—

No, you *don't!* I hollered. So I'll *tell* you! Put away the boxes! You don't need'm, hear me? We still got three weeks left! This ain't the time for acting crazy!

He just looked at me.

I got up. Put'm away! Keep'm if you want to. But

don't tape'm yet. You give me three weeks, hear me? I want'm. After that, do whatever the hell you like!

Saying that, I went out and ran crazy down the stairs to the street.

I walked up the street and beside me was trees and plots of ivy and raggy-looking weeds knee-high in vacant lots and sometimes flowers in plots in front of houses and also flowers wild and just growing up from where seeds had lit. And I was thinking, batting this reed I took out the ground at trees I passed, of how my daddy was the boy now, sitting there all tightlipped and saying nothing, just wanting to tape his boxes, like he was afraid I'd be mad if he asked, like I was the daddy now and he was the boy, needing my permission to do something he wanted to do but didn't really know hisself if it was right or wrong. And this the same man who before my mother died and he hurt his back was the strongest man I ever known and nobody ever pushed around, he wouldn't stand for it, but was all broken now and letting me talk to him in a way he'd'f once whipped my ass for so good I wouldn't't'f sat down for a week.

That's the kind of shit I was thinking about, and it weren't no fun, neither. But I kept on walking, walking through alleys all day, sometimes hidin' in garages so's not to get seen by no cop, 'cause I sure as hell didn't want to get sent home. Around sundown I saw Marvin drivin' by but I ducked down so's he wouldn't see me, 'cause I just felt too damn riled.

After it got dark I walked some more, until I was standing in the alley outside Simon Hooper's, where inside the fence that dog, Bear, was scruffin' around the yard with Hooper yelling out, *Sit!* and *Stand!* and *Go!*

It was just a joke being there, I thought, because with Daddy taping them boxes everything seemed dumb-fuckin'-stupid. I mean, why work all summer in the first place? Why do any fuckin' thing? But after Hooper took Bear in I went up a tree anyway and looked over the board fence. There was nothing. House was dark. Car weren't parked in the yard. I was just wasting my time.

But I figured, *Fuck it.* So I dropped and ran, and in no time I was outside Miss Gurpy's down on Church Lane.

It was dark in there, too, I mean no window lights. She hits the hay early I bet. So real quick I went through the side yard, ran out back, and went up them old rotty stairs. I come out through a bramble bush, and there it is. The car, I mean.

The sideviews and wipers was already fixed. Course I knew he'd do that, elseways he'd get stopped for sure, and what with selling drugs to kids he couldn't have that, so he'd took a little trip to the parts store.

I stood there about five minutes 'cause just looking at it had me feeling better, like I was doing something worthwhile. My face was all scrunched up. I was thinking about Daddy, Leezie, the house, and couldn't damn well hide it. But right then I felt my face go blank, and all the bad feelings went right out'f my mind.

I'd come up to the car. I mean I'd come out the bushes where I was hiding where no one could see me. And real slow I got down on my hands and knees, right there at the rear bumper. What I seen I could hardly believe, felt like cold air blowing through my ears. 'Cause this old car got license plates from Florida.

Florida, where Tuckie Brenner was found.

I was still crouched low when the hands grabbed my shoulders. He never said a word. He was too smart for that. All he did was try to tug me up, but like a flash I tossed back and must'f bumped him hard, smacked his nuts, maybe, 'cause he fell with a *oof!*

I never saw him. I jumped up and tore through the bushes. I tore down the hill, and I could hear him coming, smashing through the brush. But he never called out, never said a fuckin' word. I ran zigzag, and when I got to the woods I still heard him, but farther back, and he's breathing heavy. I can't yell for nobody, he'd get me faster than they could come. I gotta *hide.* So I go around a high bush right at the lip of the stream, 'bout a ten-foot drop. I jump down, hold on to the vines, and stop breathing. I'm on the wall, and it's pitch-dark. But he comes on. I hear him stop above me, and I know he's looking out. If the vine pulls free I'm fucked, I know it. I hear him breathing, and another sound, like a growl.

I don't even move my eyes. And in a minute I hear him running on, until he's far away.

I stayed there an hour. Heard the stream running under me. Never felt safe, but after a time I let go the vine and slid down until my shoes dunked in the cold water. Daddy, the house, Leezie. Never come in my mind. Took the longest, darkest way home. My head was empty 'cept one idea.

That man wanted to kill me.

CHAPTER NINETEEN

So now I was sitting in the dark.

Weren't moving at all.

Neither was Richie.

Just sitting.

Earlier what we done was cover the windows. We covered'm with cardboard and then blankets and then over the blankets we put black tarp, plastic tarp, three-ply. Then tape around the edges, taping it all down. Same sort'f tape plumbers use, duct tape.

Richie's foot's over my foot. I mean his boot's over my shoe.

But he ain't moved yet.

And we wait.

We done the windows not just for light, but for sound,

too. Light, there ain't none. None. I mean, usually in a dark room — and I've snuck around plenty of dark rooms — you wait a minute and your eyes get used to it and you can see the outlines of everything around you. But not now, because with no light there's nothing for your eye to get used to.

So you just sit.

Then you hear it.

First something off to the side, where stacks of magazines is, sounds like a flutter of pages. Then a light sort of sound, like drumming your fingers on a piece of cloth, all pitter-patter, can't hardly hear it. Then it skitters crost the floor. Then another sound, which scrapes a little. That's the dish on the floor we put out with the cream pie. But I don't hear it long, 'cause I feel Richie's boot press down and I flick the switch on that extension cord I'm holding.

Light flashes on like lightning.

That goddamn rat's surprised as we are. What it done was lurch up, its face all covered with the cream pie, and sort of look bewildered, its eyes wide. I can just barely see 'cause my eyes is blinded. But Richie, he got on them dark shades. And just then, right beside my head, I see the black line of that rifle barrel swing short and stop.

Then, *THWAT!*

And that goddamn rat is hit!

It flips so high in the air you wouldn't fuckin' believe it, and then come down all squat, splatting on the floor spreadeagle, and meantime Richie's on his feet like some goddamn commando and he's taking a step and aiming and shooting and then, *clump!* He takes another step and he aims/shoots, his eye with the sunglass over it pressed tight to the stock, whole face scrunched against the stock, elbow out sharp like some SWAT team motherfucker.

I got'm, Monkey Boy! he yells. I got'm!

You got'm, I say.

And there the damn thing is, squirming like its ass is nailed to the floor and trying to get away and sort of turning around on itself but it can't get a grip with its pink dirty hands and then—*THWAT!*—comes another shot from Richie's gun, and I'm afraid to say that's it, the poor little thing's dead as a brick, just sprawled out after a sort of twitch that made me shudder.

Hot damn, Monkey Boy! Go get'm!

Hell no! I say. I ain't picking that damn thing up!

He laughed. Shit, I'll get it, he told me.

He stepped over and bent down and got it by the tail and picked it up, and just held it there hanging dead, sort of grinning at it, pleased with what he done, and me not looking at all for but a second, when I put my hand up to block my eyes and said, Dang, Richie! I don't think it's right doing this. Ain't there a law or something?

What, law 'bout how to kill a rat? You kill'm any way you please, Monkey Boy. Ain't no law protecting rats, he said.

He's looking at it through them sunglasses he got on. He ain't wearing nothing but shorts, and with them sunglasses and his muscles and his hair bright yellow the way it is, he looks like one of them lifeguards, 'cept he got brown teeth and ain't shaved a few days. I'm keeping my eye on'm, and I can tell by how he holds it he gonna wave it in my face, so I put my arms up and say, Keep it away! Will ya chuck it?

And he did, tossing it in one'f them flip-top trash cans that got a little pedal to open the lid.

You best take that out today, I said. S'gonna stink real bad in no time.

I'll get it out, he said, and then he sat back on the chair behind me, and using a nickel, he unscrewed the screw on the back stock and pulled out the loading tube.

You know this place we was in was Miss Gurpy's attic. Had a slanted roof, and all around was boxes to the ceiling and stacks of magazines, old newspapers, too. Along the walls was old dresses hanging on nails, dust on the dresses, and hats on hooks, and other things I ain't never seen before, like skis made of wood that looked real grainy and prob'ly needed lacquer, and all sort'f other stuff 'cause Miss Gurpy, she's a lady who never throws nothing out.

The boxes I'd seen was there with the lids bust open and I got up and looked in, just sort'f wandered over like to have something to do. I picked around, seeing the sort of gloves women wear that go all the way to the elbow, made of soft leather, and stuff like eyeglasses not with frames that go behind your ears but on a sort of decorated stick, like you just hold'm over your eyes when you need'm. And there was pictures in frames, old ones, of Miss Gurpy when she was young, standing round with friends in parks and on beaches, and at school, too, it looked like, 'cause of the sorts of buildings in the background.

For a second there Richie stopped loading the gun.

Looking for something? he said.

I shook my head. Just seeing what's here, I said. I ain't taking nothing, if that's what you mean.

He gave a little laugh.

Miss Gurpy was a rich lady, he said. See that there? He nodded at a open box. That's a diamond tiara. She used to wear that to parties.

I saw what he meant and I picked it up in my hands. It was what I'd seen that night, a sort of crown piece that don't go all the way around, made of twisty strips of metal and with little jewels everywhere, big one in the front, like what you hear a genie'd wear. Some of the jewels was missing, though, just pits in the metal where they'd been.

Diamonds are fake, Monkey Boy, he said. He laughed again. Don't get any ideas.

Ain't getting any, I said. And I tossed it back, thinking how it was so busted and scraped you could never get a nickel for it — not a damn bit like what I'd hoped it was.

I kept on picking. Didn't find nothing 'cept what I'd already seen. But tell the truth, even though I was still interested in looking in the boxes, the feeling weren't as strong since getting in the attic. I'd sort'f guessed ahead of time I wouldn't see nothing I didn't know was already there, and none of it worth anything like I'd figured it might be.

But that didn't feel too bad. 'Cause I had the idea I was looking for something else now, something that would tell me more about Peter Hodsworth, and I didn't care no more about the jewels.

She was a rich lady, Richie said again, still fiddling with the rifle. My daddy told me about her. She was what you call a society dame. He looked up at me. Used to come by the place they put me when I quit drinking, Wharton Evans. He grinned. You know, nut house.

149

He looked back down again, running a cloth over the gun barrel.

She wasn't a patient, though, he said. Just visiting somebody.

Who? I said.

Some boy, he said. I didn't know him. Was in a different ward than me.

What ward? I said.

He looked at me with that twinkle he gets. Well, I was in Ward One, substance abuse. But she was always going to Ward Three.

Yeah? What's that?

He laughed short and hard. *Violent* ward, he said. Crazy motherfuckers in there, I'll tell you. I'm surprised they never locked her up too. Miss Gurpy herself, I mean. Crazy lady. 'S why she has all this junk everywhere. Take a look at'r sometime. *Close* look. You seen what she wears under her clothes? That tinfoil? She puts it there to keep spirits away, or aliens. Talk to her, you'll see what I mean. She best watch her ass, or she gonna be standing in a line every morning having a nurse stick pills in'r mouth. When I was there I could see her in the courtyard sometimes, walking through, and once I saw the boy she was coming to see with her. He had real long hair, that's all I remember.

Know his name? I said.

Never asked, Richie said.

He went back to sliding pellets in the tube.

I go on picking through the box. I was hoping now to find them coats, check out the initials wrote on'm. Didn't see'm in the boxes, so I moved the boxes aside and tipped the stacks of magazines to look behind'n see if they had fallen or was stuffed there. But they hadn't, and now I was looking back in another box at some pictures in frames, photos 'bout the size of notebook paper. I held one up.

I said, Miss Gurpy got a sister?

I don't know, Richie said.

She does, maybe, I said. Look here.

I showed him the photo. It had two girls in it, teenagers they was, standing together at some beach place, amusement pier or arcade, 'cause in the back there was some of them ball-toss games. Year was mid-1960s. I could see that from the cars.

See this girl? That's her, younger, I said. I mean it's Miss Gurpy. Looks like her.

He looked up and sort'f squinted at the picture. Yeah, he said. Never thought I'd see'r looking good as that.

Who's this other girl? I says.

Don't know, Richie says.

She's in a lot of these, I said, thumbing through the photos in the box.

Well, it ain't her sister, if that's what you mean, Richie said. Don't look like her at all.

He was right, 'cause Miss Gurpy was brown-haired, and this girl was blond, with a round face, where Miss Gurpy's was sort'f thin and narrow. But they seemed real close. I looked through the photos, and they was together in most of'm, with their arms round each other, and smiling like you never seen.

I stepped back and looked again all round the room. I figured if I just saw one more thing or just thought it all through it'd come together good and I'd get it. I sure wished I could see them coats, those initials. That'd explain it.

You know what I wish that rat's name was? Richie said. He nodded over at the trash can.

What's that? I said.

Officer Dryker, Richie said, a hard sound in his voice.

Yeah? I kept lookin' round the room.

Damn right, Richie said. I seen him following me. Last night and this morning, too. Watchin' me all the time! They got me under surveillance, I bet. Probably goes on thinking I killed those boys.

He was staring at me, his face now going all pale.

Can't worry about that fool, I said. He just got time to waste, is all.

Yeah? Well he ain't got the right to treat me this way, Richie said, sort'f groaned. Makes me feel I don't fit in around here. I swear to God, everybody's watchin' me!

He looked all crumpled up on the stool now, his head down, and I seen sweat coming out on him.

I stepped toward him. For a minute I wondered whether to tell him what I was really lookin' for, and what I'd seen going on all summer with the dark house and the boxes. I felt bad for him. But Richie, he ain't too steady, and there's no saying what he might do if I told him 'bout some of the things I'd seen.

It's all right, Richie, I said. Dryker's just a fuckin' idiot. Nobody thinks bad of you.

He lifted his face, his eyes all hollow. It worried me, seein' how bad hurt he was. And I'm thinkin' it's troubles like this gonna put him right back in that Wharton Evans if he can't live'm down.

C'mon, I said, tryin' to sound cheery. You the king of this neighborhood, everybody knows that!

He was lookin' at me, tryin' to grin and fightin' to settle himself. Then he said slowly, Yeah, I guess you're right, Monkey Boy. Well, let's get back at it.

He picked up the light, one of them cage lights on a long cord, and handed it out to me.

I didn't take it.

Hold up, I said, looking past him.

Few feet behind him I saw something poking out from behind a couple stacked boxes. Caught my eye and shook me.

Leave that light on a second, will you?

He did, and I went crost the room.

I came to what I saw. A red paper bag. Concrete. I reached down and pulled it out with both hands. The top of the bag was ripped open but it still was heavy, more'n half-full.

I stood straight and looked at Richie.

Richie, you worked for Miss Gurpy before, ain't that right?

Uh-huh.

What'd you do for'r?

She had some basement troubles. Leaks, mainly. Flood damage. Wanted it all shored up.

You use this concrete?

He looked at the bag.

Maybe, he said.

It's the sort you use, ain't it?

Yeah, he said. Quick-dry. I just troweled some in. Put it all over. But I didn't leave that bag up here. She must've brought it. I worked at'r other house.

You mean that house next to Simon Hooper?

That's the one, he said. Place was a mess. Rain got in. I fixed the floors, walls, everything. Then one night somebody came and stole all my stuff out the backyard, even my wheelbarrow. All my tools and supplies. I told her about it and she paid for everything she felt so bad, and then she paid me off. Man, I did everything in there but caulk and block out the dryer vent! I guess she liked my work, though, 'cause here I am back at it.

It was good to see that talking got his mind off Dryker. But all he said made me curious, and I squinted at him. He got up but I said, Sit a minute, Richie. I wanna talk.

He sat back down and grinned. Why you so interested? I did a little work, is all. Ain't nothing mysterious. Stop acting like it is.

I been in that house, Richie, I said. Snuck in two months ago. No one lives there.

Then nobody moved in, he said. But she owns the place.

You never saw a man come around, man 'bout your age?

He shook his head, looking funny at me, like he thought what I asked was a trick, maybe.

You ever see a man? he said.

I didn't answer that. I said, When you do this job?

Two years back, he said. Then his face sort'f scrunched

up. Funny thing is, I never brought nothing here, he said. That concrete she must've took from the other house. But she couldn't, 'cause it all was stolen. I suppose she bought that bag herself.

I can't see Miss Gurpy coming out the hardware store luggin' a ninety-pound bag of concrete, I said.

No, you're right, he said, nodding at me. Well, *somebody* bought it. C'mon. Hit the lights. We got rats to hunt.

Okay, I said.

But I didn't yet. I was too busy thinking who in hell was that man in that house, and why he keeps it so secret he's living there.

Then I froze.

I don't know if it ever happened to you, but I seen something then and it was so hard it was like getting hit in the head with a hammer, but instead of knocking me out it sort'f woke me up with a jolt, so I was more awake than I had ever been before in my life.

The room was spread around me, full of boxes and papers. But that all disappeared, and it was just me looking at that bag of concrete. It felt crazy and I didn't believe it. But what I did was nothing, and I didn't say a word.

Richie, he'd got up and was poking in that big duffle he got, looking for rounds he could put in a spare loading tube, so he didn't see me or notice anything about me. Because I was staring, and my face must'f looked crazy. But all I did was reach back and take out my wallet.

Now, I ain't really got a wallet. What I got is this sort of leather pouch with a zipper on it that I put money in when I got it, or anything I find that interests me that might be useful to me later on and'll fit inside. And what I did was unzip it and take something out. A little slip of paper. A piece of paper I'd found one morning and put in there 'cause it never felt right to just throw it away.

Then I looked back at the concrete, up around the top of the bag, where it was ripped open. On my knees I went over to it, scuffing crost the floor, and where a piece of paper was torn off the bag, I fit the piece I took out my wallet, and it fitted perfect.

I shuffled back to my chair and sat, staring at the bag. My heart was beating fast, I heard the thupping in my ears. And my mouth was dry, dry as paper.

You want to get back to it, Monkey Boy? Richie said, and he sat behind me, rifle crost his knees. C'mon, hit that light.

Sure, I said. Sure.

So I did and we sat in the dark, listening for scratches.

But I was thinking more about the bag of concrete. It was a heavy paper bag, red paper, like what they put charcoal in for barbecues. Called Masters. Masters Concrete, that's its name. But this bag, it just said ASTERS. That's all. No M. And the paper in my hand, paper I found on Tommy Evans's dead naked ass? It was a piece of red paper torn from a bag of concrete printed with a big letter *M*.

CHAPTER TWENTY

So I knew.

I knew who it was.

But I didn't know.

I knew Miss Gurpy had visited a boy in the hospital when Harrigan was there nine/ten years back, a boy in the violent ward. I knew about Peter Hodsworth, who drove that old car with Florida plates and sold drugs to boys and lived in the dark house and came and went from Miss Gurpy's out the back door, moving boxes twixt the houses, and parking his car on the hill to make sure nobody knew he was there. And I knew there was a man somewhere taking boys and killing them, who when he killed Tommy Evans didn't see a piece of paper stuck on'm that come from a bag of concrete that he went and hid in Miss Gurpy's attic.

Question was, is they all the same man?

I damn well wanted to say yes.

But I couldn't.

Because everybody knew Miss Gurpy had no son, and she didn't have no sisters, and she didn't have no visitors. Just lived alone by herself. And it could be that Hodsworth was just a man, a bad man sure who sells drugs to kids, but don't do no other wrong. And the man killing boys could be miles away in Florida.

I was so confused, I couldn't think. I had all the answers, I knew I did. Had'm right in my head, and one'f'm was the right one. I just didn't know which.

Me'n Richie, we shot rats a little while longer — well, shot at'm, 'cause we never hit none, and one, it got so scared the damn thing charged us and flipped up Richie's chest all the way like a fur ball and you should'f seen'm throw that rifle down, which busted it, and run around that room so fast, slapping at himself to get it off.

After that I left 'cause there weren't nothing else to do. And I just walked home, said no when Richie said he'd drive me, anyway he wanted to clean up.

I walked all the way. It was a little after curfew and almost dark already 'cause'f storm clouds over the houses, and I went through yards and hedges so's not to get seen. Near my house I came up the alley through the backyard.

I come round the house to the front stairs and I'm feeling the muggy heat in the air and my clothes is all sticky and I know a blow gonna come through and rain, 'cause the air's feelin' crackly on my skin. I come out on the front sidewalk there where all the bushes is, next to the community center, and I stop dead.

The car's there.

I can see through the bushes to the street, and it's parked about a hundred foot down. Skugger ain't in it, just the man. Him I see through the window and he just a sort'f clump there, all shadow.

I turn around slow and start up the sidewalk, away from my house. Don't want him to think I seen'm. But I don't even have to look back to know the car done started and's coming on after me.

I walk faster. *Skugger told'm,* I think. Then I start to run. *I messed up his car one night,* I'm thinking, *and next night he sees me at it again and chases my ass. And he'd seen me with Sam that day out front his house. So he goes asking Skugger who I am, describes me, and Skugger tells my name, and where I live.*

I look over. He's driving alongside me. Looking at me.

Just then I dart sideways through a big hedge, crashing right through and tumbling out the other side. Where I'm at now is the yard of an old couple I delivered stuff from Shatze's to, the Pheezers, and they got a old house all rundown. Round the porch is scraggly brush and half-dead bushes. I dive in. These Pheezers, they had a dog once, dog lived under the porch. Behind the bushes where you can't see is a hole busted out of the porch grating there, what you call the latticework. I crawl in under the porch. I lie still, feeling under me cold dirt. I'm smelling dirt. Listening.

I hear the brakes of the car and the door slam. I hear the bushes out front shake, and then the footfalls of a man.

And there he is. I see'm just out the opening, dungarees and work boots stomping by. *You one bold motherfucker,* I'm thinking, and I look around under the porch to see what's lying there to poke him with, rake pole or something, in case he thinks to have a look inside.

But he never seen me. Ain't a man alive gonna catch me in my own neighborhood if I got a head start, that's for damn sure. He prob'ly went straight through the yard and out the alley behind, then back around the block, 'cause a few minutes later I hear that car start up and go off slow.

He's gone but I don't move. I'm thinking. Trying to think. I figure I'll wait until it's good and dark before I risk coming out and going home.

Then a thought hits me.

I can't go home.

Fucker knows where I live, I think, *and I be damned I'm*

gonna have him coming in my window at three a.m. For all I know the fucker's sitting on my porch right now, and just the thought makes me shiver.

I can't go to the cops. What could I tell'm? Red paper wouldn't mean jack shit to nobody. I was just a boy who busted up a man's car, busted in his house, made life hell for'm. That's what they'd say. And what could I say against it? Was any cop gonna listen to me? Hell fuckin' no. Like I started telling Richie, one day 'bout a week back I'd seen Officer Dryker in the street. And I went up to him. I wanted to know what he needed from me about finding Jimmy Brest, whether I needed to give him a name or show him something, evidence, I mean. He laughed right at me. But not a good laugh, nice and friendly, but this sort of laugh that sounded sick and sharp and made me out as nothing but a liar, just nothing at all.

Billy, he said to me, *you* really *want that hundred thousand dollars, don't you?*

Hearing that made me stand still and almost forget why I'd stopped him. And he didn't wait for me to say more, but went right on, sitting there in his car where I'd come up to him, his face hard and craggy-looking, and his police cap off so his hair that's all silver was sticking up in that wave it got, and his eyes cold and blue, staring at me. And he said, *Billy, I wouldn't believe a word you say. I know what you are,* he said, *so don't come to me accusing anyone around here, or I'll have you arrested.*

A couple years back I'd of just left and maybe stole some eggs and waited on top'f some garage till he came by, and egged his ass good. But now I didn't go that route. Instead I stood a second, sort of scared of'm I ain't embarrassed to tell you, and I managed to say, *What do I need to bring you?*

How about Jimmy Brest, alive and well. Then we'll talk, okay, Billy?

His eyes still cold and blue had a sort of joke in'm, and he winked at me.

Yessir, I said.

When he pulled out I watched his car go off, and I thought, *You dumbass.* 'Cause if he'd treated me good and talked I'd prob'ly'f told him everything, how it was me who'd found Evans, even showed him the piece of red paper. But not no more. 'Cause he made it plain to me, I'd busted too many windows, stolen too many bikes, soaped too many cars.

Weren't no police for me. I was on my own.

CHAPTER TWENTY-ONE

I waited till dark, thinking every car going past was his, and wondering if he was on my porch, waiting to jump me. I thought about hiding in my yard. But if I fell asleep or made a noise he might find me, 'cause he could be coming and going all night long.

So when I come out I done something I ain't done for a year.

Crost the alley from me is Old Man Pedersen's house. He a drunk and don't do much, but as he ain't got no car what he rides is a bike, and he ain't particular about what sort, 'cause it's a girls' bike but full-size and it got those plastic strips, tassels, on the hand grips. He keeps it out back'f his house, and he don't never lock it, but just wraps the chain round it so it looks locked, prob'ly 'cause he afraid of losing the key. So what I do when I come out from under the porch is go up to that bike and unwrap the chain from round the seat, and wheel it out to the alley, real quiet. It's got a tarp tossed over it all spattered with dried paint. I take that off 'cause it's gonna rain, and I tear a hole for my head and put it over me like a poncho, and use the chain round my middle like a belt, thinking that chain might come in handy.

Then I get on and pedal.

I go down the alley and afore I gone far, the rain comes hard, hits my eyes and fills'm. I come out on the streets, looking for the car but it ain't around, and then I'm going up to the avenue where I start on fast, headed downtown, far from home as I can get.

After a few miles I pull into a gas station parking lot, the station closed down and out of business and plywood sheets nailed up over the windows. I hide a minute under the big awnings near the busted pumps in the dark, 'cause riding I couldn't see too good, and my hair was wet too, 'cause that tarp poncho don't cover my head. Didn't matter much, though. Night was warm and the rain felt good and I didn't get sick. Just hard to see, is all. Didn't see a cop around. Rain must'f put a dent in the curfew. Then I got back on and rode more.

City at night's like a big empty field, 'cept it got all them buildings in it. But they ain't got lights on, at least most don't, and there's nothing so quiet and peaceful. Like I told you, I use to ride downtown real late damn near all last summertime, 'cause it was something wild to do, and fun, too, and I used to meet all sort'f people, night people, bums and such. In the day the whole world crowds in, but at night it's like I own it, and it's all for me, with them long streets and so many streetlights the air shines bright like crystals.

Before I knew it I was through the city and past the harbor where the air smelled like rotty fish, and I was past the wharves. Rain quit and I kept going. Came into the factories, dropped my bike, and sat awhile, breathing. These is old factories I'm talking about, a whole city of'm damn near, all of'm empty and busted up, with the windows gone and no lights, and walls and roofs caved in and even trees growing up through'm 'cause no man has worked here for thirty/forty years. Sort'f place you'd never go in, even if I dared you. This a place where nobody'd ever find me, and I wouldn't see a soul.

The buildings sure was scary, big and dark, looming over me. Every little sound made me jump. *But there ain't no good in being scared,* I thought. So I got up and went in through a big hole in a wall where bricks collapsed.

I found a staircase, and I went up. I went slow 'cause I couldn't see hardly nothing. Up and up. Must'f been about the fifth floor when I saw the stairs had fallen in. All around me were drops going straight down. I felt the air rising, cold from the rain, and everywhere was just dark, dark, nothing to see 'cept little bits of the railing round where a big wide pit opened all the way down to the ground floor, like a gorge.

I sat on the edge. *Ain't nothing to be scared of,* I thought. Even squeaks from critters and groans of wind didn't bother me, and dripping water splashing far and near.

Because even then I knew there was *something.*

I mean there was something I forgot, something I *had.* Something I'd been thinking about and trying to remember ever since lying under that porch with that bastard looking for me, or even earlier when I was up in the attic with Richie after I found where the paper piece fit. Something all I had to do was look at and everything would come straight.

So I sat there in the dark with my feet hanging and my shoes wet and cold, but I couldn't damn well remember. And nothing else bothered me, or scared me, 'cept wondering what the hell it was I'd forgot, what it was I hadn't noticed when I was looking right at it.

And maybe 'cause it was so damn dark and quiet it came to me then. Like lightning. So I knew I couldn't wait till tomorrow.

I got to go home *now.*

Even if he's right there waiting for me, I got to go home.

CHAPTER TWENTY-TWO

I'll never know if he waited or not, 'cause up around Twenty-Third Street I popped a tire on a piece of glass and had to walk the damn thing the rest of the way, eight miles, and it rained again. When I finally did get home it was day and I was wet and cold and had a cough and didn't care if I saw him or not—I just figured I'd yell my ass off and run to a neighbor's. Coming in I didn't see Daddy. He was prob'ly out hunting up more boxes, and right there in the front hall I seen the ones he already had all full of stuff like a toaster and power cords and all sort of other junk from the kitchen. But that didn't bother me much. Without a place to move to, what he packed weren't going nowhere, so why worry?

I went up and lay down. Didn't even take my shoes off. I lay there and stared up. I hadn't slept in more'n thirty hours, I guessed. And I didn't sleep now. Couldn't. I'd shot rats and rode that bike all over and hardly ate, but that didn't matter.

All I could really think about was what I'd remembered sitting in the dark on them factory stairs.

But the excitement had died in me. I'd had to go home, and I'd had to walk that bike all that way through the rain, and that poncho I'd made got soaked and I was colder'n hell and with every step I took what I'd remembered seemed smaller and smaller, so nows when I'm finally in my room lying on the bed I hardly even wanna go through with it, with looking at them, I mean, 'cause now I know it ain't such a big thing and if I'm wrong I'm gonna feel like a goddamn fool.

So for five minutes I lie there, not even looking at'm.

The mittens.

'Cause I'm thinking, thinking 'bout what I'd remembered, and it was this. The first night I went in the dark house was that day I'd delivered prescriptions to Simon Hooper with Marvin and peeked in the window of the house next door. Remember that? Well, when I was standing in the house that night I had that puffy coat in my hands and unhooked the mittens. Then I tossed down the coat and looked inside the boxes with the fake jewels, which sort'f made me forget the coat, and after that I heard the man come in, but I still had the mittens in my back pocket.

But think about this. Before I tossed down the coat, I saw initials wrote on the collar, inside where the label was stitched. I remembered how I'd wanted a light to read'm but didn't have none. And that coat, I'd tried to find it at Miss Gurpy's when I was shooting rats with Richie, but it weren't there. So I'd give up on ever seeing what was wrote on it.

But sitting on them stairs in the dark I started thinking like this. If you got a mother who's so careful to write your initials on your coat collar, maybe she writes'm other places too. 'Cause like with mittens, they ain't always gonna be hooked to your coat sleeves. You take'm off, and if you leave'm somewheres you might want your initials wrote on'm, so whoever finds'm might know to bring'm right to you.

That's what I remembered. But it ain't like I was sure and I hardly wanted to look, because if I'm wrong everything I'm thinking is wrong, I mean about this man Hodsworth, and he really would be just a man whose house I busted in and whose car I busted up and in the cops' eyes has a goddamn *right* to be mad at me and chasing me around and he'd be crazy not to.

So I go on lying there until a good minute later I get

up and take them mittens in my hands. And I fold back the lower part that covers your wrist, and on the label there's wrote in black Magic Marker halfways worn out with age the letters *TB*.

I sit down. Stare at the flaky place.

Now here goes, I'm thinking.

These are Tuckie Brenner's mittens.

Was like getting hit by a truck thinking that, way it come over me.

But what did it mean?

It means Tuckie Brenner was in that house, in wintertime, when a boy might need his coat and mittens. It means he was there after he was took out'f that park where he was playing with them boys at sundown.

And right then, the other thing I forgot come to me. Here it is. There was something about Hodsworth's car, his old beat-up piece-of-shit car. I'd tried to remember it that day I was mowing Highdale's lawn but couldn't, remember? It weren't the license plate from Florida. It weren't seeing it parked at the dark house. It was something I'd heard long ago and forgot.

But now I remembered.

It was the lady cleaning her porch spars who saw Tommy Evans get took. She couldn't say about the car or truck she saw him get in, she kept saying it was one or the other. But she never said it was *both,* a car that's a pickup truck. And then I remembered something Richie'd told me about when they come for him on suspicion, saying one of their reasons was 'cause of the pickup he drives, old pickup. They thought it was maybe what the lady'd seen, the cops did, and it was one of the reasons they questioned him. But it weren't a pickup that took away Tommy Evans. It was a car *and* a pickup.

It was Peter Hodsworth's car.

My mind felt on fire and I jumped up. I'm thinking, *I'm going to the police right now because I found Tuckie Brenner's mittens and it'll help find who took'm.*

Then I sit my ass down.

What's Officer Dryker gonna ask when I get there? He'll ask, *Where'd you find the mittens?* And what do I tell'm? *Well, sir, I was breaking in this house, you see, looking to maybe find something worth money I could sell, and a man come in I couldn't see, and I come away with these mittens.*

That weren't nothing I wanted to say. 'Cause gettin' locked up wouldn't help me right about now.

And anyway, another part of me starts to wonder.

Who's TB?

Tuckie Brenner?

Maybe.

Maybe not.

I need to ask somebody if these is really his. But whoever I ask, his mother or some boy who knowed'm, they gonna wonder where I found'm.

So I can't ask. Because the second they see'm they'll call the cops and it won't be no different than me going to the cops in the first place.

I was sitting there five minutes thinking, *What the hell can I do? What's gonna be worth going to the cops and getting my ass arrested?*

Then I answer myself.

I got to put the mittens *back*. Back at Miss Gurpy's where the boxes was. I could wait till later when I was due there with Richie, but that wouldn't work for me, 'cause I needed to talk with her, with Miss Gurpy. If I done that, and found out how she knows Hodsworth and just who he is, I'd have plenty to tell the cops. And if I called the cops anonymously, sort'f crank-called'm, and told'm what I knew, but didn't say who I am, they might believe me. Or at least come check it out, same as how I once did that saying I seen a man with a shotgun going round his yard and they sent five squad cars and a helicopter, though that was just a joke, me saying that, and I laughed all day. And they'd go in Gurpy's house and if something's there they'd find it, the cops would, and I'd tell'm about the dark house too, and they'd put it all together, and I wouldn't get arrested in the deal. They could learn everything I couldn't figure out, like knowing for sure that Hodsworth lives in the dark house and hides stuff at Miss Gurpy's, and understanding why he knows her. And seeing if there's any other stuff he got that belonged to Tommy or Tuckie or Jimmy Brest in either of both the houses.

If I could tell the cops all that, it wouldn't be so bad if I *did* get arrested.

But I can't say I felt good about going there alone. Going in that house scared me.

So I lay about an hour, hoping to fall asleep and see it all go away. But I never even closed my eyes.

And when that hour was done I was back outside, walking down Denton Avenue to Gurpy's old dead-end street.

Must've been around noon.

PART THREE

CHAPTER TWENTY-THREE

She weren't home when I got there, least that's how she wanted it to look. I stood awhile out front on the walk, staring up at the house, old-looking place with them old lacquered posts made on a lathe, with trees close around it, pine trees, and them pointed roofs and that weathervane up top. I knew her tricks from making deliveries with Marvin, I mean how she might hide if she don't want visitors, so for a second I stood turned away, acting not to look at the house, but actually looking from the side of my eye, and I saw a curtain move, sort'f shake and then go still.

She was in there.

I went up on the porch. You couldn't see into the windows of'r house 'cause of the creepers, and where they was torn off there was still all this mess of them little root fingers left over, all dry and brown, and the screens was too dirty to see through. But I looked in anyway. I came all round the porch peeking in.

Finally I rung the bell, not thinking she'd answer, kind'f hoping she wouldn't. But just like that, the door opened wide and she was standing there in the dark of the house, with me looking at her through the dirty screen door.

Billy, she said, sort'f sharp-sounding and not too happy to see me. You're here so early. Where is Richie, isn't he with you?

No, ma'am, I said. I'm by myself, I said. Can I come in a minute?

Can't you stay out here? I'm very busy inside right now.

I ain't gonna bother you, I said. Richie'll be here soon. I just got to wait, is all.

She was looking at me and trying to smile but she just managed to make her face look hurt. This was funny because she'd been different yesterday, no more like a crazy lady who hollered behind closed doors when I brought her medicine, but real friendly, mainly because I guess after so many years alone she was happy to have somebody to dote on. Yesterday she'd brought snacks up to me'n Richie, and I knew it was fun for her. But now she looked at me sort'f cold for a second or two, and seeing I weren't moving away, she said, All right. Just for a minute.

He won't be long, I said, and I stepped inside.

The lights weren't on and the house was all aclutter with little tables and footstools everywhere with papers on'm, and blinds shut with only little lines of light coming out of'm, and that sort'f smell a house gets that ain't been aired in years, sour smell.

She was dressed in some sort'f dark color tight on her, and her hair, it had a net on it, black net, and I remember good how her fingernails were, all red and shiny like the paint on thumbtacks. She waved for me to come on in, even took my hand, and she said, I'll give you something to eat while you wait, bringing me into the kitchen to sit at the table while she fished in a cupboard for snacks.

I don't remember if I ever said how she looks but she's real skinny, arms like sticks, and hands, too, veiny, and a sort'f pie-crust face, all white and flaky, with the makeup painted on same as how fresh paint colors up dry dough. Figure she's seventy, or roundabouts.

I was trying to look happy, and as she peeked at me now and again from behind cabinet doors I tried to smile but couldn't, and she saw I was feeling maybe a little nervous and her face got dark.

What's the matter, Billy? she asked.

I swear, way her voice creaks, sounds like cellophane.

Nothing, ma'am, I said, sittin' there, hands on my lap. Just gotta talk with you, is all. Will you sit awhile?

She stopped and looked at me, holding a tin of cookies in her hand. Her face was sort'f stiff and she set the tin on the table.

Will Richie be here soon? she said. She didn't sit like I asked but kept busy jerking around for them little plates and napkins old ladies use, going in these glass-face drawers to get'm. She seemed real nervous, that like even though she'd let me in to stay what she really wanted was to chuck me out the door right now. And I seen when she weren't looking my way, she was peeking at the kitchen door behind me.

Richie ain't coming, I said. Will you sit with me? I gotta ask you something.

She stopped and froze, looking at me. She didn't say nothing but just pulled a chair out and sat, sort'f careful, her back real straight and her hair and glasses wiry and her face old and white. And that tinfoil Richie talked about, to keep the aliens away? I looked then and seen it under the lip of her collar.

Just as she sat she said, I need to get you some milk, and she started to stand, but right then I looked up'n said, Do you have a son, Miss Gurpy?

She stopped moving. And something come into her face.

Fear.

'Cause from the way she stared I could see I'd just asked the worst thing in the world.

Do you, Miss Gurpy? I said, looking up at'r. A son? Or maybe a nephew? Or just some boy you know and took care of? He'd be about Richie's age now, I'm thinkin'. D'you have anybody like that?

I heard the water dripping in the sink. And I saw her eyes behind her glasses get bigger and rounder, and it was like we was trying to see who could stare longest.

Then she yelled, *No!*

But that no meant yes.

I said, Richie told me when he was at Wharton Evans you used to come by visiting somebody, boy about his age, but he didn't know'm. Who was that boy, Miss Gurpy?

As I talked her face looked to stretch over its bones, and her eyes got bright and splintery, and her mouth twitchy like she wanted to move her lips but couldn't, and she bit the bottom one, it all pasty-red, and the lipstick got on'r teeth.

I found something upstairs here, I said. I think this boy of yours done some bad things. So I got to know who he is. You gotta tell me. It might save some people's lives. I mean it. I found things that make me sure, but I can't prove it. Will you tell me, Miss Gurpy? Will you, please?

This kitchen we was in was dim like the rest of the house but all the furniture, the fridge and table and counters, was all old and white and boxy, catching the little light there was. Doorway was hung with those sort'f beads hanging down on strings. I was watching Miss Gurpy, waiting for her to answer me. Her face was afraid and she was looking at me, but then I heard the beads in the doorway click, and she looked up fast behind me.

I turned quick and Peter Hodsworth come in the room.

The first thing I wanted was to run, just leap from the chair and run out'f there. But he come right up to me, one big step, and I knew no matter how fast I jumped he'd get me. So I just kept sitting, and I watched him.

He was looking at Miss Gurpy, his eyes cold and shaking his head real slow side to side, like he was saying she'd done something wrong, but not with any words. Then he looked down at me and saw me watchin' him, so suddenly he smiled real big, like he's happy to see me, and he says, Hey, man, are you Billy Zeets? I've been dying to meet you!

I told him I was. And right then he drops a hand on

my shoulder. I looked tight on him. He kept his big smile and his eyes looked bright and frozen on me.

He says, real cheerful, Are you here to do some work? Place sure needs it, huh? He's still smiling, and asking real nice. My aunt told me you were getting the rats in the attic! Gross, huh? It sort'f freaked me out! She didn't tell me until last night, and I've got some stuff in there I don't want messed up. Really *important* stuff. It's not cool she didn't tell me, huh? She's a little wacked, huh? And again he looked at her like she'd done wrong.

I didn't say nothing. I felt the mittens stuffed in my back pocket. And I knew now I'd never get'm upstairs like I'd wanted, so I could go 'head and call the police.

Miss Gurpy suddenly said, He's waiting for Richie Harrigan, Peter.

She said it fast and loud, and a little wild, like somehow she had the terrors. What I ain't said is, the whole time she seemed awful scared of'm, jerking herself whenever she moved like a hit might be coming, and never saying a word 'cept to blurt it real sudden.

He just looked at her and grinned.

No. Richie's not coming. I heard Billy say that.

He smiled down at me again, squeezed my shoulder.

Miss Gurpy's mouth twitched. She didn't say nothing.

Hodsworth said to me, Well, are you done here? C'mon! I'll drive you home.

Don't need it, brung my bike, I lied.

We'll take it along! he said.

I didn't say nothing for a minute. He was looking down at me and never took his hand off my shoulder, like he'd caught me. And even though he had a smile on his face, there was something in his eyes that weren't a smile.

All right, I said.

He looked at Miss Gurpy and said, I'll be back in a few hours. Come on, Billy, he said, and I got up and went to the back door, me walking first and him right behind me.

CHAPTER TWENTY-FOUR

Tell the truth, I can't remember too good what all happened after we left the house. I mean, a lot of people have asked me what it was like to drive with Peter Hodsworth and talk with'm, and did he act all nutty, and was it sort'f like a cat-and-mouse game where he asked me questions to see how much I knowed. But the way it went none of that sort of thing happened. He pretty much just started beatin' on me right away.

That ain't totally true, though. He did ask a *few* questions, 'cause there was one thing he wanted to know from me. But once he got that, the other thing started, and I can't remember too good at all.

Now, you know how Miss Gurpy's house was at a dead end, last house, and then woods for a ways. Out back was the big yard all run over with vines and high grass she never cut, and then the big hill with the narrow flight of wooden stairs going up it, the stairs all rotty and busted and the banister just this long line of two-by-fours fallen off the posts and buried in the grass.

Like I said, I was walking first and Hodsworth walked right behind me. His hand was still on my shoulder and he weren't letting go. And halfway up he put on the other hand, holding tight, and shoved a couple times to keep me moving.

He said, Go up the stairs, Billy. My car's up there.

I thought about running. But right then my legs felt funny. Hard to move, even to go up the stairs. I knew Hodsworth ain't slow, knew it from when he'd chased me the other night, and I'd escaped just 'cause I knew the woods better. He was big, too, sort'f chunky. Almost fat. But he could move, and was strong, and I couldn't out-run'm, 'specially 'cause I was tired and so scared I could hardly move.

When we got up top I was breathing hard but he weren't. There weren't no street, but just that alley of beat-down grass, trees so thick on both sides they rose up high and made a tunnel. His car was there, parked in the shade. *A car that's a truck,* I thought.

He went ahead of me a pace and stopped. A sort'f grin come over his face, not a nice one. He said to me, Hey, looks like we forgot your bike . . .

But from how he talked I knew he hadn't forgot nothing.

Well, he said, that's no problem, man. We'll zip around front for it! C'mon, he said, and opened the door. Hop in!

I did. He sort'f shoved me there, then he shut the door and locked it. Then he went around his side and got in and started it. He pulled out in reverse, crackling over the twigs, brambles scratching 'longside the car. We was sitting side by side, 'cause there only two seats in that Ranchero.

For a second he stopped.

When we're out there on the street, Billy, I want you to keep your head down. It's best no one sees you with me. Okay?

He waited a second, and then grinned at me again.

C'mon! he says. All the other kids do it. Really, it'll be cool!

He talked all cheerful but there was something in his eyes I didn't want to argue with. So I said okay and slunk down a bit, till my head was same level with the doorjamb.

That's good, Billy, he said, and backed up farther out the alley.

We drove, him looking forward, and we went through streets making quick turns. He didn't talk no more, didn't look over at me, neither. We never stopped out front Miss Gurpy's house for any bike of mine. Some drizzle come and he turned the wipers on, going *swap-swap*. From where my head was I could look up'n see the sky full of dark clouds and treetops, and when we'd been going straight awhile I knew we was on the avenue.

After a few minutes he turned into some backroads that go into the woods if you stay on'm long enough, up near Robert E. Lee Park, top'f the avenue. All the while he's looking forward out the windshield paying no mind to me, and I see he got a smile on his face, all sort'f crimped'n sneaky-looking, and now'n then his cheek jerks almost like he's talking, like he got a voice running on in his head.

This ain't the way to go, I says.

It ain't? he says.

No, it *ain't,* I say.

I thought it's pretty early, he said. Let's drive somewhere. We've never hung out before. You've never even driven with me. It's time you did.

Where we goin'? I said.

Let's go to the park, he said. Let's catch a buzz!

This last he said not like he was offerin', but was something he hisself was looking forward to.

He keeps going. Don't turn. Finally we go down a long hill through trees with leaves all wet and drippy and then onto a dirt trail with busted timber at the sides and the road all gone to mud, and from how I sat I could feel the tires digging in but not deep enough to stall us. We went far down the trail, all the way to that watershed place where boys take their girlfriends and there're all sorts of ghost stories about.

He pulled into a quiet little lane near where you could see the concrete wall of a power plant, and then he stopped the car and turned the wipers off too. Me, I'm looking over at him. He reaches in 's pocket, takes out a baggy full of weed, and fills a pipe he got out the dashboard ashtray.

I watch him.

I don't smoke none of that, I say. Never did.

No? he says. Grins at me, then flicks the lighter he got, and the smoke rises from the little metal pipe sticking out his mouth.

Yeah, I got work to do today, I say. If you ain't gonna take me home I oughta walk. I'm in a hurry. Can I get out?

I reached for the door lever, thinking that when he'd

turned off the car it'd opened the locks. But right then he flicked that switch on his armrest and locked my door again, and there weren't no button to pull for me to open it.

He don't look at me. But he says, No, you can't get out.

In one big huff he smokes that bowl, then taps it out in the ashtray, holding the smoke in a long while. Then he lets it go with a bigger huff and looks at me, his eyes all full'f questions.

He said, Why are you following me around, Billy? Why are you spying on me?

I ain't, I say.

He breathed out, kind'f long and impatient, and looked ahead, and looked back at me, and smiled then, and laughed without laughin', 'cause the sound it made was all anger.

You know, I asked around about you. I had to find out who you are. The other boys say you do a lot of fucked-up things. They don't like you much. They say their parents hate you and you can't go in their houses . . . So first I thought maybe you were just fuckin' around with me, breaking my stuff and wanting to rob me like you do to everyone else. But that's not right, is it? I heard what you said to my aunt. You said I do bad things. What bad things,

Billy? And you said you found things to prove it. What? You *know* something about me. What do you know?

I'm looking up out the window. Rain's come again and it's splashing down like hose water, jiggling the leaves. I'm gettin' antsy lookin' at'm, the jiggling leaves, I mean, and I start shoving at the door even though I know I can't open it and he sees me plain as day.

Let me the fuck out'f this car! I say.

I start yanking at it and real fast he reaches at me and puts a hand on my shoulder'n shoves me. I jump my ass back on my side and stare at the fucker.

I said somewhere I was scared. Think I said that. But it ain't so. There ain't no word for what I was. *Scared* is maybe when a rabid dog comes up and barks and you gotta run your ass away, and it chases snapping at your ass and maybe it gets you or maybe it don't. But that ain't what I was. I was a thousand times more. Best I can put it was like holding a live wire, the current running through you so hard you can't move or think and can't even piss your pants, 'cause it ain't electricity coming through you but terror itself. You know, like little kids? I was like a little kid who screams when you hurt'm, screams with crazy terror, even though I weren't screaming just yet. But even a little kid got a brain, but it was like I didn't have one, and so was more like a cat you got chased in a corner and'r whacking at, and it's all arched up with something more than terror and the look in its eyes is like it sees right into hell.

That's how I look. And I gotta say he was surprised. For a second he smiles, saying, *Relax,* Billy! I'm not going to *hurt* you. *Nothing's* happening.

For a minute I said nothing. Big brown leaves lay flat on the windshield, rain running round'm. Fucker's getting weird on me, his face all googly and wild, starin', and gettin' shaky.

He says, Why are you following me around?

I *ain't,* I say.

Tell me, Billy.

I ain't! I yell, looking at'm.

Do you want to get out of this car?

Yes!

Then tell me!

I sat dazed and staring and then I mumbled something 'cause I'm dumb enough to think maybe he really meant what he said. But he don't hear me, so he says, What's that, and I yell, *To see what the fuck you was doin'!*

He says, What *was* I doing?

I say, Nothing.

He goes to reach for his lighter again, but instead he sort'f lurches over. He beats my face against the window and I scream loud. In a second he grabbed me, smacked me on the door. Lay hard on me, face up close.

Listen, you little shit, tell me what you've seen. I'll make you!

After that I can't get straight anything. I had blood in my eyes and mouth and up my nose and I was crying. He was shaking me real hard, thumping me, and my head was knocking everywhere. I'm crying and yelling and he's yelling, asking what I seen, what I know about'm. And then he sits up and lights another bowl of that weed and lets me lie there. I try to talk but my voice won't let me. I was crying like a kid and sort'f begging, and I said, *Let me out and I'll tell.* Said it over and over.

And when he said he would I told him.

I don't know if it made sense to'm, and I can't remember how I went at it 'cause I was blubbery with blood and snot and my face all wet, but I told how I was in the house when he was there, how I found the mittens, saw the boxes, messed his car, everything, even about Tommy Evans and the paper piece, I told it all. I didn't look at'm and he didn't move.

His face sort'f emptied. Went plain. Nothing at all. But such rage in his eyes. I ain't never seen it before. And he's pulled away from me like what I'm saying has been hitting against him, pressing him back against the door on his side, his arms out and his hands all spidery, grabbing the seats, 'cause me, I'm scaring the shit out'f him, and he don't know yet what to do.

Then he says, sort'f stutters, his eyes all splintery, Who else knows, Billy?

I cried, *Nobody!*

He laughed at that, looked real happy. Said, You haven't *told* anyone?

I can't think and I'm crying. I yell, *I told my daddy, I told my daddy!*

All this time I'm looking round the car. Trash is everywhere. But I didn't see no pens or pencils, nothing sharp. There ain't nothing made of glass, nothing made of metal.

He's saying I didn't tell but I yell I did, that I told Daddy to call the cops if I ain't back soon. I couldn't really talk 'cause I hurt so bad, and I was confused 'cause I was also trying to look all round the car, down near my legs and feet to see what might be lying there.

I told my daddy! I told my daddy! I yell.

No, you didn't, Billy, he says.

I'd hit the dashboard when he smacked me around, and the glove compartment fell open. Right inside it in a mess of papers I see a screwdriver.

I was shaking and he saw it. He smiled, leaning at me.

I couldn't move. Turned my eyes to'm.

How did you find out, Billy?

I yelled.

I yelled as long and loud as I could, right in his face, and he jerked back, looking like I'd shot him. Then I jammed forward, tore at the glove compartment, and ripped through faster than I ever done. Right then like a miracle I had that screwdriver in my hand, and I was leaning over at him, jabbing it at his eyes.

He caught my hand and tore it lose. Then he looked at me his face all horrible and yelled, *YOU LITTLE SHIT!*

I felt the first time my head hit the doorjamb, but not all them other times.

CHAPTER TWENTY-FIVE

I woke up sitting on a chair in a dark room. My head hurt and for a while I couldn't open my eyes, and I just sat there. I was crying, I could feel that. And my pants was wet. I pissed'm, ain't sorry to say. Didn't know where the fuck I was, scuze my language. All I knew was that my arms and legs hurt because I was tied to the chair, and the rope was biting real deep into my wrists and my legs. I could tell my face was all fucked up, not just 'cause it hurt, but I could feel it all swollen, like a dough lump sitting on my face, kind'f stretching it over, know what I mean? And all round my mouth was tape, prob'ly duct tape, wound round maybe four/five times, so I couldn't make a sound.

I couldn't just remember all what happened. Last

196

thing that came to me was walking down to Gurpy's house, but then slowly in my head it all came back, and I could see myself at the table with'r, and Hodsworth showing up, and us in the car, and him talking and hitting. But after that it weren't so clear like I say, 'cept I knew I'd told him everything.

I got an eye open. What I could see, sort'f half-see 'cause my eye would only go half-open, was my lap and the floor, just a brown, bare wood floor. But there was so much blood on my lap I started to cry again.

How the fuck had this happened to me?

Scuze my language.

I think a minute passed, more like five or ten. Though it hurt a lot I raised my head and got both eyes open. Room was dark. There was a bed there, almost behind me, I could just barely see it. Windows were covered, some sort of wood sheet, nailed up. A closet, and a box of drawers, one drawer open, empty. That was it. Like a house nobody lives in.

Downstairs, I ain't said this but it'd been happening all along, was noises. Somebody was creeping around. Moving things. I heard the wood creak like it does in empty houses made of wood, and them creaks went everywhere, creaking the ceiling and the walls, too, 'cause there weren't nothing to muffle it, no carpets. Made me glad I hadn't moved. 'Cause I thought it was prob'ly the fucker down-stairs, Hodsworth, I mean, and I'll be damned if I wanted him to hear me.

Now I'll say what happened next. There was sound on the stairs, foot stomps. Then in the hall outside, I figured it was a hall out there, and it was, I seen later.

Then the door banged open.

I let my head drop. I can't tell you how I felt. You can't know. But what happened, all that happened, was the fucker came crost the floor, grabbed ahold my hair, the front of it, and jerked my head up. Like I said, my eyes was closed, and no matter that it hurt so much, I did not move a muscle, and didn't make a sound.

Fucker could'f punched me and I wouldn't'f moved.

That's how scared I felt.

But none of that mattered. Fucker thought I was dead, is what it was. Looking back now I know he did.

I thought he'd slit my throat, and for some reason in my head I was saying, *Go 'head, fucker, go 'head, fucker,* over'n over, not 'cause I wanted it, but thinking that made me brave.

But all the fucker did, once he thought I was dead, was drop my head and go back out the door. It shut and I heard him lock it. I still didn't move or open my eyes, even though I heard him going back down the stairs. But then I heard something good, the front door slam way down there, and then a minute later a car start.

I couldn't fuckin' believe it.

He was *gone!*

I looked over best I could, and from out the corner of my eye I saw there was a blanket piled on the bed. And right there, 'cause I could see better now, was a boy's hand sticking out under it.

There was a boy on the goddamn bed!

I didn't fuckin' move, and then, though it hurt like hell, I tried to jerk around.

But nothing budged.

I looked round the room again. Looked at everything. I was waiting. In my head I felt cold, don't know how else to say it. Had to feel cold. Was the only way to get out of there. My eyes went skimming over the door, the closet, the crisscross of shadows on the floorboards. I was looking for something I knew would be there. I was waiting to see it. Waiting for it to come along.

And even though I had that tape crost my mouth, I laughed.

I was done pissing my pants and crying, and I kept looking around and I was thinking. Thinking cold, because

I knew what he was gonna do. I was thinking that the motherfucker thinks he's smart 'cause he tied me to a chair and there ain't no lights and the window is boarded, but the motherfucker didn't think of who I am. He didn't think how a boy who spent half his life busting in houses sure as hell could bust his way out, and thinking that and just about laughing at the fucker, 'cept maybe I was still crying, I was looking around to see what I could use to get the fuck out of there.

And then I seen it.

A nail poking up out the floor, its shadow crossin' the lines of the floorboards, making a neat little X. Not no regular nail, neither. Big nail, one of them flooring nails, big fuckin' hunk of steel.

It took me a minute to knock myself over, but with jerking my shoulders I went down with a big crash. And when I did that, the chair broke. Chair back broke off the seat. Fucker hadn't counted on that! And that made the ropes a little loose on my legs, 'cause they was tied around the chair legs, which had shifted. So what I did then, by sort of churning my ass, was get over to that flooring nail.

I don't know how long it took. When I got to it, it was behind my back, and it was hell getting that nail on the rope, which was nylon cord and hard to cut.

I scraped at the nail, gouging at it, and it was hard goin' 'cause that rope was so tight I couldn't feel my hands. But I felt the strands breaking. I kept yanking, and after maybe five minutes, they were off.

My hands were blue'n cut to shreds and I had to rub'm together for a long while before I could get the cord off my legs. All the while I kept saying, *Come on, fucker, come on, fucker,* 'cause it made me feel bold. And then I was on my feet, rope off me, and the tape off my mouth.

I was thinking how to get out when like from nowhere I look at the boy on the bed. There he was, on his back. Like I said, his hand was poking out of the blanket. Funny thing was, where most times a blanket rises up over your chest, on this boy, the blanket sunk low. I didn't know what to make of that. And without thinking I went over and pulled it back.

I been sayin' I was scared. Ain't true. Whatever I'd felt earlier was nothing.

All I'm gonna say is the boy was dead. But what had been done to him I ain't never seen before, even in a butcher shop.

I tossed the blanket back and turned away fast. I was shaking and mumbling, and in my head I was saying, *The window the window the window,* 'cause there was that covered window about eight foot away. And looking at it I grabbed up a piece of that chair, and using the chair leg and the nylon cord, I busted down the wood on the window, which was nothing but a sheet of Masonite, the thick kind.

It took me another minute to bash out the glass. Then I bashed out the frame. And then I was out that window and sitting on the roof under an eave, looking down into Simon Hooper's backyard.

But I didn't go nowhere, just sat.

I was so beat to shit I was 'fraid to climb down. I knew I might fall. So I was sitting. And it was still light out there, looked about six or seven, sun was starting to go down, maybe, and I could see the woods far over the tops of the houses, and next door was Simon Hooper's like I said, and everything was quiet. Breeze was blowing over me, and I heard birds.

What happened to that boy was the worst I'd ever seen, even worse than Tommy Evans, and that was bad enough. And even though my head was beat so bad I was dopey, I knew there was other boys in the house. Dead or alive, they was there.

And what could I do?

I could maybe climb down. Maybe get a neighbor or a cop. But they all knew me, knew me the same as Dryker did, and I couldn't say if they'd believe me, even beat up like I was. None of'm liked me or trusted me one bit, 'cept maybe to steal what they got on their porches.

But anyway, that weren't even it. What mattered most was the motherfucker.

Hodsworth, I mean.

'Cause he went out.

And when he came back and didn't find me, and knew I'd seen the dead boy, who was the boy they later learned was from Georgia 'cause I ain't never seen him before, well, when the motherfucker saw that, what would he do?

He'd kill'm all. That is, kill'm if they was still alive.

I felt scared now with what I was thinking, 'cause I was scared to go back in there and look for the boys, and I knew I couldn't do it, didn't have the heart, and I cried.

Then I turned around and got on my knees and pulled out a piece of wood from the window, piece of frame 'bout ten inches long, and stuck with broken glass caulked in tight that didn't bust out when I'd hit it with the chair leg. Figured it might hold.

I knew the door inside was locked with a bolt so I had to pick another window that would let me into a different room. That was easy, just a slide over the roof. Before going I made the sign of the cross, while I was looking in at the dead boy.

Then I slid on over.

Window was locked, one of them swivel locks screwed to the top of the lower frame, in there behind the glass. So what I done was take that frame piece and poke out a little glass in front of that swivel lock, and it broke pretty clean and quiet.

Then I reached my fingers in, turned the swivel, raised the sash, and went inside.

CHAPTER TWENTY-SIX

Where I was weren't a room but a stairway, and I was at the top on the landing looking down the stairs, which was narrow and had no carpet on'm and led steep down to a shut door. I held that piece of frame up and out, pointed like a dagger, sharp glass on it rising up sort'f like a fish fin, and I went down.

Door down there was unlocked and I swung it slow and even, but 'it still creaked. Every step I took cracked and echoed 'cause there weren't no carpet and no furniture anywhere to muffle nothing. Every little sound seemed loud enough to shake the house, but I went on, so scared I was damn near falling on my face.

I didn't know what the hell I was doing. I was just looking for boys, and didn't know where they was. I moved real slow, bobbing my legs up and down, same as how my daddy used to walk coming home late from the bars. So with that frame piece raised high like a butcher knife, there I was creeping, my face all bumpy-blue and bloody, and I must'f looked crazy.

I went through halls and saw nothing, 'cept here and there a cardboard box of junk in an empty room or a chest of drawers with no drawers in it prob'ly drug in from an alley nearby, but nothing nowhere else. Food wrappers on the floor, and beer cans. I did see a mattress with no sheets and no blanket in one room, front room, prob'ly also drug from an alley. But there weren't no lights inside, just what come in the windows in some of the rooms, and most of the windows was covered, so it was everywhere dark.

Then a new room come up I looked in, and in there was a box and I looked in it.

I saw vials.

Lots of'm, like maybe two/three hundred. Medicine vials, I mean, like Doc Shatze hands out, orange with white caps. It was all I found. But that made sense to me, 'cause I knew the motherfucker sold'm to the kids, so's here's his stash, I figured.

It felt like hours was going by and I was crazy scared and I was going on, knowing I was losing time. I heard sometimes a car outside come by slow and I froze waiting to hear it pull up but one never did, and I breathed again. And I started thinking I was wrong comin' back in and there was no one in here, and it was like my ass started itchin' and my legs got all trembly just wanting to run the hell out.

But then I stopped.

I thought of something.

I was down on the first floor then, I'd been all through the third and second.

What did Richie say?

The basement. The cellar. He'd worked on it. Shored up wherever leaks was with concrete, places water might get in, 'cause Miss Gurpy said she was 'fraid of floods. And he'd done it, so he said, till his gear all got took, including that bag of concrete we found at Miss Gurpy's.

So that was it.

Down there.

If a boy was here, that had to be the place, 'cause it'd be all solid with concrete over everything, and like a prison.

I went back through a hall and into the kitchen, and there on the wall was a door. It had a big bolt, a slider. That's all. No padlock, and nothing needing a key. But on it there was a key ring on a nail, and I figured it was prob'ly for doors down there, doors that needed keys. So

I took it, the key ring. And then I pulled the slider and opened the door.

I ain't gonna tell you 'bout the smell that come up 'cept to say you don't want to smell it. That was the first thing I saw, I mean noticed. It was all dark down there, but here's a thing. There was one of them utility lights hanging from the ceiling by a cord, hanging right there over the stairs, kind'f light with a plastic cage over the bulb, yellow plastic. So I unhooked it. Had to hop up to do that. And now I got it in my hand. I flicked it, and on it went. I put the frame piece under my arm, careful not to cut myself, and I held my nose. And taking the steps one at a time, went down slow.

Basement weren't like upstairs, there was lots of stuff in it. Lots of boxes. A big table was there, old one, and another table upended on top'f it, and between the legs there was lots more boxes. I didn't look'n the boxes. Some sawhorses was around too, I remember that. Against the wall, stone wall, all painted white and made'f big lumpy stones with mortar churning out'f'm, was a washer and a dryer still with the exhaust tube coming up out the back and fixed to a window. The window was painted white, or nailed over in white board, it was too dark to tell which. But I knew the washer and dryer was busted, 'cause the doors was gone on both of'm, and inside where the clothes go was full'f trash. Otherwise I seen the ceiling was covered with lots of rusty metal pipes for water and such, and there was posts made of the same lumpy stones holding up the ceiling, and I seen all this with that utility light I was holding, and the back door, too, which had boxes scattered near it on the floor, maybe ready to be took outside.

But none of that was what I wanted to find. I was looking for locks, and when I got to the back of the basement there was an old door made'f heavy planks and big heavy iron cross brackets fixed with rivets, and on it was three big padlocks, and I stopped. I didn't want to move, and the smell was so bad there it made my eyes water.

I flashed the light on the locks and seen they was all bright silver and new, and they was all made by the same company. So I flashed the light on the key ring and found the three new keys with the same name.

This room I was looking at, it was where you might put your lawn tools, your mower and such. That's what the room was.

I stood there another minute because I couldn't open it up yet. I didn't want to. I didn't want to see that boy on the bed, or nothing like'm.

But when that minute was done I took the keys and

one by one opened the locks and unhitched'm, and tossed'm down. Then I held my breath and swung the door wide and put the light in, and there was Jimmy Brest sitting a yard away, tied to a widow's chair, staring at me.

He was alive.

CHAPTER TWENTY-SEVEN

I ain't gonna tell you nothing about how he looked, or if he was wearing anything, or most'f what he said. If you wanna know so bad go ask'm yourself, or go read what the police made me tell'm. What I will say is when he first saw me he didn't have no idea who I was, or how the hell I could be there, but when I told'm, and I had to tell'm six/seven times 'cause that's where he was at, he started calling me names again.

Can you believe that fucking shit?

All he could manage was a mumble, and his mouth weren't taped over 'cause he could yell his head off in there and not get heard. And mumbling like he did, his head lolling low and his chin on his chest, arms tied behind him, he was cussing me like I said.

At first I just thought he'd gone crazy, and I ignored him 'cept to say I had to cut the ropes. But then something came into my head and I understood. So I knelt right beside him and I put my mouth right up to his ear and I said, Jimmy, I ain't with Hodsworth. You get me? I ain't here for'm. You see my face, he beat me, too. I'm here to get you out, boy. So quit cussin' me.

I had to say that maybe ten times. And when he finally got it he looked at me. And long as I live I will never forget the look he had. I'm standing here trying to tell you how it was, but I can't. A human being don't get that look. Sometimes a dog does. I mean a dog at the pound when it knows what's coming, and if I ever see't again I'll die.

I told him I had something to cut the ropes with and I did, setting the light on the floor so it aimed up and using the glass best I could not to cut him, 'cause the rope was so tight his hands and feet was black and purple. When I got the ropes out, 'cause they was stuck in 's skin, I had to rub his wrists and ankles a good five minutes afore he had feeling in'm.

All this time he ain't saying nothing. His head hangs low and spit comes out his mouth, and he sort'f moans a little, but he can't talk. And when I got the ropes off he don't get up but just pitches forward real sudden on the floor. And then when I try to get him on his feet I gotta heft him on my shoulder 'cause he can't stand up. That weren't hard for me, 'cause I figured he weighed maybe thirty/forty pounds less than when I last seen'm, and was skinnier'n me now.

Jimmy, I says, you gotta help me. You gotta think.

I'm walking along here, his arm over my shoulder, and I left the light in the room 'cause I couldn't carry it, and my frame piece too, 'cause I forgot it. So I couldn't see that good 'cause the light was going away, blocked by all the junk on the tables. I wanted to get'm to the stairs, 'cause the back door looked too hard to get at with them boxes on the floor, 'specially in the dark.

We slogged along, and then I leaned over for balance. But when he looked up and saw the stairs he started yelling. I mean yelling, even though he had no strength to yell so it come out his mouth all busted, and he was looking up the stairway like it was hell and he tore his arms off me and grabbed the railings, and stood there froze.

Christ Almighty! You gotta quit it! I said, and I stuffed my hands over his mouth, and by getting my face right up in his, and staring at him without blinking, I got him to simmer down, though his eyes still was filled with terror. What it was he was afraid of upstairs I couldn't say, but if it was anything like that boy I seen on the bed I understood why he wouldn't go up.

I said, Okay, we ain't going there. We gonna go out the back. But you be quiet, now. He ain't here. But we can't let'm hear us if he comes back. Now come with me.

It took maybe five more minutes to get'm to the back door because I was tired now and he fell twice and I had to pick'm up. I was dizzy, too, and sick from the air down there, and I was feeling afraid 'cause I was getting weak, too weak to move. Coming to the door I had to lean Jimmy against the wall so's I could push aside the boxes scattered on the floor. And after I done that, I felt even worse, because I seen that door was locked from outside.

Not just locked, but had this thing on it I seen in hardware stores, a sort of slide lock made of steel bars, vault lock, that go all crost the door on gears and needs a special key.

For a minute I fiddled with it, what I could see of't in the dark, but it was no use.

I can't do it, Jimmy! I said, yanking at it. I gotta go upstairs! There's another door. I'll just be a minute —

He yelled when I said all that, even louder than before.

I looked at Jimmy and said nothing. His face was so full of fear and he was shaking, and he stood by hisself a second and he took my hands and held'm, and was staring at me his face all scrambled and his mouth mumbling, and I heard him *praying* to me, you understand? And when I saw that I said, I ain't going nowhere, Jimmy. I staying with you, you hear? Don't you worry none, you hear?

He squeezed my hands tight, and I saw there a little bit of a smile come on his face, and he cried, standing there.

That made me feel good a second, but that didn't matter. 'Cause right then we heard a rap outside, and more noises, and then the bolt on that door shot across, and it flew open, letting in the last of the sunlight outside.

What happened next went by so fast it's hard to say just what it was. I was standing there with Jimmy beside me, and that back door came open, swinging at us, and Hodsworth was standing outside about two foot away. He shoved the door hard and it hit me, but I caught it with my hand. Then he came up fast and smacked me just about as hard as he could, and I whammed back against the wall, but I didn't let go'f the door.

Jimmy just stood there. But when Hodsworth hit me he had to step forward, and when he did, Jimmy walked right past him, right outside into the backyard. Hodsworth was gonna hit me again, but when he saw Jimmy outside he backed up out the door to grab him. And taking him in one hand he turned toward me and fished in his pocket with the other, and pulled a gun and aimed it at my face.

Now the only reason I'm standing here talking is because right then Jimmy did something.

He pushed'm.

He pushed'm just as he shot, and that bullet missed me, and Hodsworth had to drop his hand from Jimmy and grab at the doorway to steady hisself. I never knew if Jimmy meant to save me. I mean, maybe he just wanted to walk farther outside. But he pushed, really sort'f fell on'm, and that's what saved my life.

Because I had a second. And you gotta remember that even though the fucker smacked me good, I still was holding on to that open door.

So I slammed it. He was just outside the door'n I wanted to lock him out. Which was lucky for me. 'Cause I didn't see where his hand was. It was in the doorjamb, holding on the steel slot for the lock, steel about an inch thick, solid. And when that door slammed it crushed that fucker's hand flat between the bolt and the slot, and that fucker yelled like the end of the world, I mean howled like a motherfucker you ain't never heard before.

I wanted to run, but the fucker was standing in the doorway and I was afraid to get near'm, 'specially as how he still had that gun in his hand and every move he made was like he was thrashing around, so I couldn't get by. And the whole world seemed crazy, so who could think? Because like I said, I can't really remember just what happened, I mean in the order it did. All I know is I was lying there on the cold concrete 'cause I'd fell down, and Hodsworth was there in the doorway with twilight all round him, and Jimmy Brest, he was in the backyard just wandering around naked as a jaybird and with so many cuts on'm it looked like somebody'd been at'm with a hacksaw.

Then the fucker hit me again. Somehow he got over the pain long enough to just jump at me, and kick me so hard I flew crost the floor. But it was worse for him. I don't know if it was 'cause he just moved his hand or banged it, but that fucker yelled so loud after that it was to wake the dead, and then he just keeps up this roaring, roaring like I only heard animals do, and he comes to stomp me but he can't 'cause just lifting his foot over my head makes him scream again, and if I weren't screaming and crying then I'd bet I'd'f laughed in the fucker's face, 'cause the way he moved was like a country boy two-step. And he's trying to bash me but he's holding his wrist to keep his hand still, he stuck the pistol in his pocket I guess, and that damn hand, you oughta'f seen it. It was swelled up like you wouldn't believe, like some cartoon hand or just 'bout the size of a catcher's mitt, and I ain't lying. 'Cept it ain't that tan color a catcher's mitt has but all white and blue, and the gash in the middle went straight through, 'cause I forgot to tell you how it got stuck on the slot piece when I slammed it and he had to yank it free and I heard this sort'f *doink!* when he done that and then he screamed again, that gash all black and horrible and blood just squirting out like juice from a squishy orange.

Then the fucker does the weirdest thing. Instead of going after me he just slams the door, bashes it shut, and the last I seen of the outside was that Jimmy Brest had found the gate and looked to be walking into the purple of the alley. So it was dark except for the light I'd left in the storage room, and by that light Hodsworth was bashing at boxes I'd pushed away from the door, trying to open'm with his hand but when that hurt too much he bends down to rip the flaps open with his teeth, and after he does he thrashes his good hand through, and comes up with pill vials. He can't open'm so he busts'm under his foot and then he starts taking these damn pills, down on his knees, whole fuckin' handfuls of'm. And then he finds hisself some bag of powder, and I figure it's either heroin or cocaine, 'cause what he does is rip the plastic with his teeth, and still jerking around 'cause he can't stand the pain, I mean moving like some weird robot man, he starts to pour the stuff over 's hand, so it clouds the air and I smell it a little too. And if you're wondering why I ain't doing much it's 'cause I got hurt when he kicked me, but now with me thinking he might get the pain to go away I get to my feet and go toward the stairs.

He was aiming to shoot me again, raising up his hand to level the gun at me. But any little move he made hurt like hell 'cause it made him move that busted hand, and even bump it, which really made'm holler. So he'd move and then scream and jerk and then move again and scream louder, and the gun went off and the shot hit the wall. I was stumbling away, to where I didn't know, and he was lurching and jerking behind me. And all the time sucking them pills out the vial to kill the pain.

And that's when the fucker shot me, back of my right leg, right there high on the big muscle.

God damn.

I fell down just as the flash cracked like lightning and so loud in that little room, and the powder smell black and bad, and my head hit the floor hard 'cause I fell backwards and I didn't move.

And when I looked up, there the fucker was, right over me, gun aimed down at my head.

And that was it.

'Cept one thing.

When I looked up, I could barely just see his face, a feeling came over me I don't even want to talk about.

But I guess I got to.

But I don't know if I can.

It was like, *I hate you more'n you hate me.* And, *I'd kill the world to kill you, fucker.* And it was, *Fucker, burn in hell.*

And thinkin' that way I scare myself now, 'cause I never had it in me to kill nobody, never wanted it or thought I could go that far. But for what he'd done to them boys this fucker was the devil himself. He deserved to die, and I was damn well glad to be the one try'n to do it. 'Cause sorry to say, right then I was maybe more'f a monster'n he was.

So I managed to lift a foot and boot the fucker's fucked-up hand.

Boy did he yell.

But it didn't matter much. He still shot me in the belly. Went straight through.

He wandered off screaming, I didn't see where. I just lay on the floor.

I was done. I knew it. I didn't think but just waited, my mind so full of pain I couldn't think. And he was coming to me, he fell down and was crawling over the floor dragging hisself with the good hand, the other held up high, and I closed my eyes to die.

And now you gonna think I'm crazy.

'Cause I looked over and right there my mother was standing in the basement, three/four yards away. And I didn't understand because she couldn't be there. She was dead, for one thing, so why did I see her ghost? But she was there and looking at me, dressed in that old flower dress I remember, her hair done up with pins. And seeing her made me so happy I swear I forgot about the pain because I just wanted to tell her, tell her what we was doing since she'd gone and the house and me trying to make the money, and Daddy wanting his fruit stand, and Leezie and her baby. But even more I wanted to say to her all the things I wished I'd ever said but never did, 'cause I was too proud to say'm, even to her. And I did say'm, right then on the floor, said'm all without talking, because I didn't have to talk. But I knew she heard me just the same, standing there looking down at me.

But she didn't seem to care. She just looked at me, her face sort'f dark, and she said, Billy, get up.

But I was too excited for that and I said, Mommy, can't you hear? And I said the things again, all about the fruit stand and Leezie and the house, and how I loved her and felt sad she was gone but had been too afraid to ever tell.

She said, Get up, Billy.

I felt bad. She didn't answer me. She didn't care. I

wanted to ask her if she loved me too and about what I was doing now and Leezie and the fruit stand and if those things was good to do, and I wanted to tell her I weren't bad no more like she'd begged me to be, but I couldn't ask no more 'cause I was crying.

And she said, Get up, Billy.

I said, Mommy, I can't.

I was crying.

Get up, she said.

Mommy, I'm hurt, I told'r.

She said, You can, Billy. Get up, Billy. Get up and run.

Mommy, I can't, I said.

So she said, Listen, Billy. Listen.

And then I knew my eyes was closed all along, 'cause I opened them, and she weren't there no more.

But I listened. And I heard what she wanted me to.

So I sat up.

Because I knew now I had a chance. I didn't see a way out yet, or even know if there was one, 'cause the door was shut and Hodsworth lay between me and it, crawling my way. But I knew why I had to get up and run like she said. Because I heard the one thing that could save me.

Then something busted inside when I moved and blood came out my mouth and down my chin.

I knew I was gonna die. There weren't gonna be

nothing. And I knowed I'd never get my daddy a fruit stand and never see Leezie's baby. I'd never see any of it 'cause I knew I'd die.

But then I stopped.

My mind stopped.

Because I weren't talking to Mommy no more.

I was talking to God.

And I said, I know you hate me. I know I'm going to hell like them nuns at school say.

So okay, I said.

I'll go.

Just let me deserve it.

You just let me kill this motherfucker, I said. Let me get up and kill the motherfucker. Just gimme five minutes. And show me the way. Then I'll deserve it. It's worth it then and you can go 'head and put me there.

And I felt I could ask'm, 'cause what I heard.

A dog bark and a boy's voice, Simon Hooper, yelling, *At it, Bear,* and *Down!*

So I got up.

I don't know how. 'Cause I weren't thinking but remembering, remembering now 'cause the Lord put it there. And Richie, he'd said he'd shored up the walls and floors with concrete and everything against the floods Miss Gurpy was worried 'bout, but he ain't done one window, 'cause all his stuff got stole, Hodsworth stole it, and Miss Gurpy let Richie go without getting it done.

So I knew dryers had them exhaust shafts of wire and foil, and this one was sticking right to a four-frame window that maybe was painted glass and not hardboard. 'Cause Richie had told me hisself he never changed it, sealed it, finished it, and this asshole motherfucker crawling at me screaming with a gun in his hand sure as hell never done it hisself.

So I climbed onto the dryer and not even thinking put my face right through that wall that smashed open 'cause it was glass not board and I clawed hard, feeling glass cutting my arms straight to the bone, and feeling that motherfucker now standing, grabbing my legs, and I kicked back and must'f hit that big hand 'cause he screamed crazy, and I pulled hard and squirmed fast and I was out.

It was still daytime sort'f, still purple-dark, and I was in a yard standing on grass. I heard him inside coming out smashing everything in his way. So I went forward. Didn't walk. Hobbled and looked, and there in the fence was that tree trunk, fence built around it, and the old wood blocks nailed on, for boys to climb to the tree fort in the boughs. So I climbed up and slumped on the fence top.

And right then the fucker come up and shot me in the back.

I don't remember falling. Just hitting the ground woke me and I lay where I hit. I saw the motherfucker jump down and there he was in front of me 'cause he'd climbed after me. And them pain pills was working 'cause his big hand hung low and he was aiming the gun at my face.

I didn't say, but falling I hit my head and my eyes went dizzy. I was seeing three/four things when really there just was one. And in my ears was a sound like thunder, like rain, and I couldn't hear no other sounds. Everything was moving slow and three/four times over, and my face in a pile of acorn mulch sort'f steaming, and dead leaves, just the last things I wanted to smell.

And I saw Hodsworth standing there, four/five guns in his four/five arms.

But he weren't looking at me.

He was looking at Simon Hooper and his dog.

I looked too.

Bear was sort'f pitched forward, with Hooper right beside him, holding'm by the scruff of the neck. And Hooper looked at me and then he looked at Hodsworth, and his face didn't so much change as go dark. Then he raised his hand and pointed at Hodsworth and drew his hand, whipped it, crost his own throat, 'cept I saw three/four hands doing it, and he said something sharp, yelled it, but I couldn't hear 'cause'f the roaring in my ears.

Hodsworth didn't move. He couldn't. All he did was jerk his eyes because that dog jumped and toppled him down like somebody'd throwed a big dirty rug all crost him.

But I didn't see no more.

I fainted.

And I'm glad.

'Cause I seen that dog bite off a tree branch size of your arm, and when it was done that motherfucker didn't have a neck no more.

CHAPTER TWENTY-EIGHT

After that I was asleep nine weeks.

I know you all know about that. Nobody thought I'd wake up, and the only reason I got there at all was because of the ambulance man, paramedic man, who tied tourniquets on me lying there on the ground and fixed me up with a transfusion, Simon Hooper standing right there with'm holding the blood bag in his hand, and Bear right there too. I'm happy they hadn't shot Bear. You think they would'f, with all them cops in the yard. You'd think one of'm would'f plugged'm, 'specially with a dead man lying on the ground he just killed. But they didn't, though that's usually what a dog'll get when he puts a man down. But to hear Simon Hooper tell it — he came by the other day and talked awhile, told me all this I'm sayin' — old Bear just gave them cops the jollies, and when they was getting me up in the ambulance one of'm went over and started patting his head and said he wanted to buy him a T-bone. Damndest thing.

Nobody knew my blood type and why would they, but they had this type O negative, universal blood type, they said, and it kept me going till I got crost town. I'd been shot in the back, shot through the gut, shot in the leg. I had four ribs broken, fractured skull, busted collarbone, busted wrist, cuts and bruises. Lost, they say, more blood than should'f killed me. My face was all purple and black and when they got me down there, hospital, they cleaned me up and wrapped me up, and Leezie says my face didn't even look like a face but a sort of big purple and black balloon, and my whole body was wrapped over double in so much gauze and plaster cast and all trussed up with cords like I was hogtied.

Some people ask me if I remember anything from being asleep so long.

I got to say no.

But what I tell'm is that the usual thing when you fall asleep is you start to dream, and when you wake up, that dream is done.

But me, it worked the other way.

'Cause I didn't dream none at all when I was sleeping. But when I woke up, life was like a dream.

Because that's when they all started coming. I mean all of'm. Colonel Brest and Mr. Harrigan and Officer Dryker and Marvin and Richie and parents I never met and everybody. And other people I did not know, like the governor, and even people from television coming by so much they had to throw'm out.

But I didn't see'm, I was asleep, and it was Leezie and Sam Tate who did the talking for me, though there weren't that much they knew.

The police found out everything about Peter Hodsworth, and Miss Gurpy, too, and all that about him being her friend's son who was born out'f her knowing some rich man who was already married, and how she died when he was born, Miss Gurpy's friend, I mean, so Miss Gurpy raised'm, to keep that rich man from taking him away. But she didn't like him 'cause by killing his mother getting born he killed the only person she ever loved, so she said. But she'd promised to raise him, in secret, too, so the rich man never knew, and now everybody talks about how in the places she put'm things was done to'm that made'm crazy like he was. But me, I don't believe that last part, 'cause I had some nasties done to me, 'specially back when my daddy was drinking, and even though I took a few in my time you don't see me going and killing nobody.

I was trying to remember when I'd first seen'm, and I think it was four years back. I'll tell you what he was. He was a man who hung with boys. He knew the boys in the neighborhood who got rich parents and smoke a lot'f weed and do other drugs.

There're other guys his age who hang with boys. Richie Harrigan's one of'm. It looks natural, because they still act like boys, ain't too different, but they got more money 'cause maybe they got a job and they got cars'n stuff, and it's fun to hang with'm, 'specially when they got the best drugs and that sort of stuff, and always have something to drink, liquor, I mean. Me, I don't do drugs or drink, but a lot of boys do, and for them, Peter Hodsworth is just about the coolest friend in the world to have.

And that's the thing, 'cause he weren't from around here. He was from Florida, lived down there most of the year, and just come up north a month or two now and again. So when the police went around questioning people, after Tommy Evans got took, they never questioned him, because they had no record of him, and no boy ever mentioned his name. And anyway he prob'ly weren't even around, but down in Florida, living in that trailer they say he had.

'Member that boy Skugger? He was Hodsworth's

boy, Skugger was, and Hodsworth never laid a hand on'm. Skugger didn't know nothing about what Hodsworth really did. He was just Hodsworth's friend and got to know him, and Hodsworth gave him drugs for free, and pretty soon Skugger, he needed those drugs every day, and to keep getting'm for free he'd introduce Hodsworth to all his friends, boys like Tommy Evans and Tuckie Brenner and Jimmy Brest, and together they'd all meet in secret places and have parties and get high. And since Hodsworth knew these boys was taking drugs they never mentioned his name to the police when they was asked if they knew anybody who they think might'f been taking the boys, because first, they didn't think it was him, 'cause he acted like a friend, and second, he'd'f talked and said things to get'm all in trouble and chucked out of school.

But what Skugger never knew was sometimes Hodsworth spotted a boy alone, like Tommy or Tuckie or Jimmy Brest, and he'd ask'm in the car if he knew for sure no one was watching, and he'd ask'm to keep their head down just like he asked me, 'cause he'd tell'm he was taking'm somewheres to get high. And the place he took'm was his house next to Simon Hooper's, which Miss Gurpy had bought for'm, a place from where they'd never come back.

He didn't have no idea what was really going on,

Skugger, I mean. He was just sort'f like Hodsworth's stooge, and made Hodsworth look like a friend of the boys and not the one killing'm.

But I know you know all that, and prob'ly more'n me, 'cause I don't watch them news shows.

Miss Gurpy, they didn't do nothing to her but put her in the hospital, that place where Richie'd been, Wharton Evans, and that's because she weren't complicitous, as some people called it, meaning that she never helped him catch the boys, but that he'd scared her so much and threatened to kill'r so many times she did whatever he wanted. And what with who she was already, being half-crazy herself since her friend died, and with all her mess in her house and that tinfoil under'r dress and other craziness, nobody really could blame her as a killer, though they did put her up like I said, and forever.

And that fake jewelry she had, and them dresses and gloves? They gave her some of that, 'cause she called it her memories and begged'm for it, begged her doctors, sayin' it was all that was left of her past, and they was the things Hodsworth took away from'r to hurt her if she didn't do just exactly what he wanted. For all I know she's walking around Wharton Evans right now dressed up like she was forty years ago at them beaches and parties with'r friend.

I know you know about Hodsworth and what he done

to the boys, and I ain't gonna tell you any more 'bout what he done to'm when they was alive. I told enough.

One thing I gotta say is they found two other boys in that house. I went through all the rooms, like I said, but didn't even see'm, but that's 'cause where they was, which was in those sort'f ceiling cubbies you got in some houses, crawlways in the ceilings you only get to through little trapdoors too hard to see in the dark. And both them boys lived too, though one was in the hospital almost long as me.

But they found a lot of dead boys too. I mean pieces of'm.

One'f them boys was from Georgia, boy on the bed, and there was lots of boys I never knowed from states all over because to not get caught Hodsworth would mix it up and grab boys wherever, out of state. When he was done with'm, and killed'm, he'd drive out and dump'm, sometimes close to home, like where I found Tommy Evans, sometimes Florida, like he done Tuckie Brenner, sometimes other places. They'll never find'm all. They don't even know how many boys he took, but it was many. Because in his rooms they found things that put it back eight/nine years he been doing this, or more, ever since Miss Gurpy took him out of Wharton Evans and put him up in the house that nobody knowed she owned.

Damn I'm tired.

Scuze my language.

Anyway, when they first come I didn't see'm 'cause I was still knocked out. Then I come to and I was so achy and yelling all the time they didn't let nobody in and I was on painkillers all day all night, and all trussed up for two months more. There was so many cards they took'm and put'm in a book, nurses did, one'f them photo-album books, 'cause they was in the way of the wires. Best is from Marvin, one where he wrote down I got triple luck. That's funny, I wanna talk to'm 'bout that. I turned fifteen lying there, and Leezie, she wanted to throw me a party but I said I weren't up for it. But I got more presents dropped off than ever before in my life. Flowers, too, everywhere you looked. And one thing I'll say is if you sick, there ain't nothing worse to have around than flowers, just the wrong smell to have. But thank you all anyway, that was real nice of you.

Anyway I'm all right. Got a tic. Arm sort'f flinches now and again, got it they say getting hit in the head, hitting it when I fell off the fence or maybe on the doorjamb. But they say it might go 'way, you never know. Anyway it ain't so bad, not like Mrs. Murphy's son, who fell out a tree making a fort when he was seven and hit his head on a stone, and got all palsied after that, and now's damn near forty and works up Lowry's grocery store and can't help but pull your hair when he goes to pat your head.

CHAPTER TWENTY-NINE

I was home a week when they came, I mean Colonel Brest
and Mr. Harrigan. You gotta remember what I said about
Richie, I'm sure you do, 'bout how he got arrested on
suspicion and really was under twenty-four-hour surveillance just like he thought, and was worried 'bout his rep-
utation, him having been a drunk and all, and gettin' so
nervous his daddy was set to put him back in Wharton
Evans. But now all that was thrown out, as they say,
'cause everybody knew Richie had nothing at all to do
with the crimes.

Mr. Harrigan was real happy that what I found cleared
his son, and while I was asleep he'd talked to my daddy and
done some things, and so had Colonel Brest, and like I said,
it was about a week after I come home that they come by to

tell me about it, figuring that was long enough for me to feel better and not get riled by what they say.

They was downstairs, it was noon I think, and they asked if I could come down but Leezie, she told how I couldn't walk the stairs yet, so they come up. It was Mr. Harrigan who come in first, and then Colonel Brest and then Daddy. Daddy, he was smiling. I ain't seen that for a year'r more and I was glad. Can't say how much glad. But I knew something was up, and then Daddy, he told me that these was the fathers of Jimmy Brest and Richie Harrigan, that they had some things to tell me.

Mr. Harrigan, he wore what you see'm in at the bank, suit sort'f silver gray, and he a hard-looking man. Chunky-looking, boxy, and got silver hair like his suit, same color, and a face I swear's like a stone and don't smile much never. But I'm trying to tell you how his face looked that day and it looked like I can't tell you. 'Cause I ain't never seen that look before. It was like he was so glad 'bout what I'd done, he wanted to smile but his face looked hard and stiff 'cause he weren't used to being glad, or at least showing it on his face, so his smile was sort'f busted up and sort'f trembly, if you get what I mean. I mean a smile was there, but sort'f stuffed in there and was having trouble getting out. Still, I could see without him even talking that what he wanted to do was maybe grab me or something, hug me, I mean, and that's the best I can say.

Anyway, what he did say was, Billy, while you were in a coma Colonel Brest and I cleared up a few financial difficulties your family has been having.

Then my daddy says, yells, really, That's right, Billy! They bought back the house! He smiled big sayin' that.

Mr. Harrigan looked a little surprised at my daddy just blurtin' out like that, and then looked back at me on the bed.

Yes, he said. What your father says is correct, Billy.

I tell you, the way he talked was funny, so serious and straight.

Then he said, The house has been completely restored to your father's possession. It is his, fee simple, which means —

That means it's *all* mine, Billy! Daddy said. I don't owe *nothing!* That loan I got was bad, Mr. Harrigan found that out!

Daddy clapped his hands then, and Mr. Harrigan, he grinned just a little.

Yes, it had some discrepancies, Billy, he said.

I felt confused, so I sat up and looked at him.

Now, you gotta know something. This Mr. Harrigan

was a man who'd never talked to me before and never would'f, 'cept maybe to say I belonged in jail or the boys' home. And now here he is with Colonel Brest, who before was just the same about me, and they in my room, and telling me all these things.

So I gotta tell you.

I felt embarrassed.

'Cause sitting there hearing this, all I could think about was how a year back I went and tossed a paint bag on Mr. Harrigan's car. Mercedes car. New one. Right there in the parking lot outside his bank. Oil paint, too, primer, red as a cherry, and hard to get off.

So now I looked at Mr. Harrigan and I tell you my face must'f been red like the paint and I said, Mr. Harrigan I just want to say I'm sorry for what I done to your car a year back. Be honest, just being here with you makes me a little embarrassed, sir. I mean, doing that with a paint bag, that was real dumb of me, and I'm sorry.

He looked down at me. His face didn't even change. He just said, Billy, I've forgotten what you did to my car. You probably had your reasons, anyway. I believe on a previous occasion I was rude to your father when he came to the bank to discuss some financial matters with me. I believe it is I who owe you and your father an apology. I give that apology now. I am truly sorry for what I said. I assure you that it will never happen again.

I mean, yeah, he meant a time a year or so back when he throwed my daddy out the bank. Daddy'd come in asking for money or to complain about that house loan, I forget which, and Mr. Harrigan, he'd cussed'm and tossed'm out, and that did rile me, I s'pose, which had me chucking that paint.

But Mr. Harrigan was looking at me, ain't took 's eyes off me. He says, Billy, no price can be put on what you have done. For my son, and for the Colonel's. You must understand that.

I was staring at'm. What the hell could I say to that?

I said, Thank you.

Once Mr. Harrigan was through telling me 'bout all he done, he shook my hand and my daddy's and said he was needing to get back to the bank, and he shook the Colonel's hand too, but the Colonel said, to me and my daddy, said, I'd like to stay a moment longer and have a word alone with Billy, if that's all right with you, sir.

He called my daddy sir, he did.

My daddy, he said, Sure.

And then it was just the Colonel and me, and we was alone in my room.

Now I ain't said it, but the Colonel, he was all got-up like for a parade. Had on his dress uniform, they call it, with one of them hats like a cop wears, 'cept with gold and silver on it, and gold and silver on his uniform, too, and shiny shoes all black, and enough little colored plaques on his breast pinned there and enough medals and bars to make your head spin. And I forgot to say, too, but all this time he had a box in his hands, nice-looking box, closed with a sort of silver clasp.

But he didn't say nothing at first. Just stood there looking at me.

He was biting his lip to make his mouth still, and his eyes were almost gonna cry, but not with sadness, with something else. I mean his face was sort'f shaky.

He said, Billy, when you woke in the house, you broke out and could have run home. Is that true?

I said, Yessir.

But you went back in the house and found my son, even though that man had beaten you for over an hour?

He was starting to cry and I couldn't look at him. I said, Yessir.

He said, Billy, there are some people . . .

Then he couldn't go on.

Second later he looked right at me and started again, said, Billy, once I saved a few men and was given a medal.

Some people might think the same thing could never happen to you. I won't allow that.

He opened the box in his hands and took out a medal on a string, ribbon sort of string. Star-shaped medal. He come over to me and looped it over my head. Then he stepped back. I'm presenting you this, son, for acts of uncommon valor. I used to think I knew what courage is. You have improved my understanding.

He stood straight and saluted me.

God damn.

I looked at the medal, looked down at it hanging there. Then I looked at him'n said, Thank you, sir. And I saluted him back, which made him happy, I guess, 'cause I seen him smile a bit.

We didn't say nothing then. And me, I thought about some things I'd heard.

Fact is, I knew that the Colonel never really took to his son Jimmy. Up my way, you always hear that kind'f thing about people, families, 'cause nosy people talk, saying he liked better the one named David, or Davey, like he was called, who died in the war, but really 'cause he got sick on a transport boat. And people knew now how Jimmy bopped my nose that day with that basketball, because you know how Richie said a neighbor lady said she seen him beat Jimmy up and told Dryker? Well that same lady talked now about how Brest had hit me, which she'd seen and knew about all along but never thought to tell until just now.

So thinking about what really happened that day in the house, I said, Sir, I don't really think I deserve this. Jimmy, your boy, some people have said nasty things about him, said he didn't stay like I did. But he didn't run away from me. You gotta know that. He come back just like me and he pushed'm. And he ain't done that, I wouldn't be here, that's for sure and I know it. He'd been in that hellhole for weeks with that nut, you gotta understand that. Me, I'd only been there a few hours, that's all. You gotta know he was brave, sir. You gotta understand that.

Colonel Brest, he didn't say nothing for a minute, but I seen a little light in his eyes.

Then he said, Billy, I've known grown men afraid to do what you have done.

No, sir, I said. They'd'f done it. I weren't all that brave, honest. You just had to be there. Anybody would'f, 'cause there weren't no other way.

He crooked a smile then, like he knew something somewhere behind what I said that I didn't even know myself. Then he said, nodding his head and his eyes bright like he was looking not just at me but at a whole bunch of people, said, Billy, they all say that.

Then he come up a foot and looked down right at me.

Billy, he said, Mr. Harrigan and I have talked. We intend to give you anything you want. It's all we can do.

I raised my hands open at the sides.

I got a hundred grand, sir. I don't need nothing.

It's all we can do, he said.

Okay, I said, seeing he was dead set on it. I'll think about it.

He was waiting.

How about a bike, I said.

That's not enough, he said.

What's enough?

I'll be judge of that, he said.

I said, Um, hmm.

He was quiet a minute, looking at me, then he said something, and I could tell it was something he was waiting to say all along.

When you are a bit older, I can have you enrolled in officers' training school, if that interests you. You would make a fine officer, Billy, I am certain. I would provide the highest recommendation for you. We want to ensure that neither you nor anyone in your family ever finds themselves in a difficult situation again. Some boys are born to privileges you have not had. It would be my privilege were you to allow me to give them to you.

Damn. I had to think a minute.

Well, sir, I said, I appreciate that, and I'd do it, but see, I'm a little busted up from what went on, and might not get in for that. Got this tic and all? But really, you see, I got this idea about me'n my daddy, working together, doing something like that. That's what he wants, Daddy, I mean, my mother, too, afore she died, so I figure it's what's best for me.

Now I was confused, everything coming all at once, but that offer there, it got me thinking. I mean, that ain't just something you throw away.

So I said, Well, sir, you know about my sister, how she was feeling bad about all that was happening and got herself pregnant? I know it don't excuse nothing, but she was just feeling bad.

Yes, Billy, he said.

Well, the boy who's the father, he ain't a good boy. His name's Ricky, Bad-Ass Ricky, we all call him, scuze my language, and he —

I know who he is, Billy, the Colonel said. What about him?

Well, way he acts, he just gonna wind up in jail, and that ain't good for Leezie or the baby. So I was thinking about this offer you makin' me, that training school?

He don't say nothing but I see a look come in 's eyes. Sort'f smiling look.

Then I realize I'm smiling too, and really about to laugh out loud, 'cause I say, Well, way I see it is *he* oughta be the one to go. He's thinks he's real tough and maybe he is, and that training school'd prob'ly keep him outta trouble, know what I mean?

That Colonel, now he got a big smile on his face, and I see it.

So I say, barely say, 'cause I'm laughin', Could you imagine him in officers' training school? Them drill instructors? Oh, that'd be funny! Oh, that'd be *rich!*

By this time we're laughin' and I'm laughin' and he's laughin' and he got tears on his face 'cause that's where his feelings went. And I swear to God, I'm laughin'.

Billy, I—I—I'll see what I can do! he says.

Then he straightens hisself up and says, But Billy, that's still not for you.

I felt a little shy. Really didn't want nothin'. The house was fine. Leezie was gonna be okay 'cause they said they was getting her a nanny so she could stay in school, forgot to say that. Even that dumbass Ricky was gonna be fine, though I can hardly think 'bout the shit he'll go through.

I had the goddamn Congressional Medal of Honor, for God's sake.

'Cause that's what it is.

Then it hit me.

Something I'd thought about so much I'd damned well forgot it. Something that had been on my mind for months and that I'd thought of over and over, and is prob'ly the only reason I been saying this lying here flat on my ass in bed, talking into this recorder Sam Tate loaned me yesterday, digital recorder that don't even need no tape but just records anything you say for hours and hours, sixteen straight hours, like it says on the box.

'Cause I was thinking 'bout my daddy, how he fell off that roof and how he could never pay and almost lost the house and had nothing left to do.

So I looked up bright.

Well, sir, there is one thing. It's kind'f complicated. And might be a little expensive.

He did look a little nervous.

But he cracked another smile anyway.

CHAPTER THIRTY

Well there you go.

That's how my daddy got his fruit stand.

One funny thing I'll tell you is I'm lying here in my room talking into this thing Sam loaned me, and I guess it's around eight now because the sun's down outside and the pole lights just came on over the community center lot. And anyway, just a minute ago who comes knocking but Leezie.

She says, Billy?

I say, Yar?

And she opens the door, pops her head in. You hungry now? I made you something.

Me, I say no because I don't want to stop. I gotta finish this, Leezie, then I'll come, I say.

Leezie, she come all the way in now and stands over my bed. You want the light on? she says. I say no 'cause I like the light coming in from the pole lights.

How 'bout your pain pills?

Took'm, I say.

Leezie visits every day to make my food and I say, How can you, with your belly big like that? But she flushed red like to smack me and said, I'm here to make you dinner every day. And I said, seeing her so mad to do it, I guess you are. She says, Don't you want me to be nice to you? I say, Sure, if you feel good about it. She says, I do. Now standing there, she says, Where you at telling? 'Cause I already told her everything and she knows, so I say, Just a few minutes more. She thinks a sec and says, All righty. You call for me, then?

I say, Yar.

You gotta see how pretty her face is. Real clean-looking and young, 'cause of this baby she don't eat much but vegetables and drinks this water outta bottles like she read to do in a magazine, so the baby's never sick. Quit smoking just like that, and ain't drunk a drop, neither, and neither has that fool Bad-Ass, 'cause she don't let'm. She bosses that boy like a two-year-old just like she said she would. And if he don't do what she says, his brothers — and they even tougher than he is — they on his ass in a minute.

Don't that make you laugh? Me, I'm laughing right now.

She's standing there with the hall light behind her, and I ain't never seen her looking so pretty. And how she walks out the door, that's why I stopped to tell you this. Way she walks makes you so happy you could cry, 'cause that poor girl can hardly walk, and waddles like a big ole duck, and gotta turn sideways, 'cause my door is stuck and never could open all the way.

The Colonel and Mr. Harrigan, they both put up the money for the stand. Store, really. I told'm no. Said just show us the way, I'd use the hundred thousand, but they said that was my money, and meant just for me. So what they done was take my daddy down to City Hall for papers and permits and all that, and then helped him find just the right sort'f place to have the store, which was easy for them 'cause they know everybody in real estate, and buy all the whatnot of what he needs to keep the fruit and everything else, truck, too. So now what they doing is working on the sign, which gonna have Daddy's name on it, and my name on it, and so I guess that's that, that's everything, 'cept what I maybe forgot.

'Cause there're some things I can't remember that I know I'll never forget. I mean things I can't remember 'cause they're way down buried in my head, but where?

And some people, they want to know why I done what I done, I mean what kept me going, 'specially after I got hurt so bad. But to find that out I'd have to dig down so deep in myself there'd be nothing left but darkness, and I can't go there. I'd have to ask the dark, and I can't do that, 'cause the dark don't answer.

But what I said's enough.

'Cause I been talking into this thing Sam brought me since noontime, eight hours now, and I'm tired like I said. But you got all what I did, and that's everything.

And if I left anything out it'd just be so's not to scare nobody, as I get scared myself sometimes. 'Cause I won't go out to no dark place no more come nothing, and can't hardly tell you the chill I get when I jerk awake alone at night, dreaming I'm standing at the top of them basement stairs, back inside that dark house.

ACKNOWLEDGMENTS

I owe the life of this book:

To my wife, Alma, and son, Hugo, whose constant love is my greatest support.

To my agent, Dan Lazar at Writers House, whose keen eye found Billy his best home.

To Anne Hoppe, editor extraordinaire at Clarion, who always let Billy speak for himself, and whose suggestions helped me make his voice even truer.

To my teacher, the great novelist John Rechy, whose special light showed me what I can do.

And to my wonderful father, brother, sister and late mother, who made me what I am, and gave me what I try to express.

These people made *Ask the Dark* possible and inevitable. They put this book in your hands. They have my deepest gratitude. I thank them all.